To Woo a Widow
Heart of a Duke Series

For more information about the author:
www.christicaldwellauthor.com
christicaldwellauthor@gmail.com
Twitter: @ChristiCaldwell
Or on Facebook at: Christi Caldwell Author

For first glimpse at covers, excerpts, and free bonus material, be sure to sign up for my monthly newsletter!
Printed in the USA.

Cover Design and Interior Format

To Woo a Widow

Heart
of a
Duke

THE
SERIES

USA Today Bestseller

CHRISTI CALDWELL

Other Titles by
Christi Caldwell

THE HEART OF A SCANDAL
In Need of a Knight—Prequel Novella
Schooling the Duke
Heart of a Duke
In Need of a Duke—Prequel Novella
For Love of the Duke
More than a Duke
The Love of a Rogue
Loved by a Duke
To Love a Lord
The Heart of a Scoundrel
To Wed His Christmas Lady
To Trust a Rogue
The Lure of a Rake
To Woo a Widow

LORDS OF HONOR
Seduced by a Lady's Heart
Captivated by a Lady's Charm
Rescued by a Lady's Love
Tempted by a Lady's Smile

SCANDALOUS SEASONS
Forever Betrothed, Never the Bride
Never Courted, Suddenly Wed
Always Proper, Suddenly Scandalous
Always a Rogue, Forever Her Love
A Marquess for Christmas
Once a Wallflower, at Last His Love

SINFUL BRIDES
The Rogue's Wager
The Scoundrel's Honor

THE THEODOSIA SWORD
Only for His Lady

DANBY
A Season of Hope
Winning a Lady's Heart

BRETHREN OF THE LORDS
My Lady of Deception
Memoir: Non-Fiction
Uninterrupted Joy

CHAPTER 1

London, England
Late Spring 1818

"*Everyone knows fairytales include A charming prince, an always smiling, hopeful princess, and a joyous happily ever after. This story is very much the same…*"

A soft sigh interrupted Philippa, Lady Winston's reading. Seated in the nursery, with one daughter balanced on her lap and the other at her feet, Philippa glanced up from the small leather book.

On the lips of her five-year-old daughter, Faith, hovered a dreamy smile. "What happens next?" The girl, stretched out on her belly, kicked her legs up behind her.

Knowing the tale inside out, Philippa closed the book and spoke in soft tones, careful to position her lips so that her daughter could see them. "This princess, however, was unlike any of the other princesses…"

Her daughter rounded her eyes. "Can she not hear out of one ear like me, Mama?" Philippa's heart pulled. "Or is she a widow like you?"

Philippa jerked and the book tumbled to the floor where it landed with a soft thump. Where she had always been guarded in her thoughts and emotions, there was an unrestrained honesty to Faith that, as a mother, she found both pride and awe in. On some occasions, *many* of them to be precise, Philippa found herself disconcerted by her daughter's stream of questionings.

Faith quickly retrieved the volume and waved it about. "Can a widow be a princess in a book?" she continued on a rush. "Because Grandmother was whispering to Lady Martindale and Lady Martindale said that widows were old, gray, plump, and never married." She brightened a bit. "I know because I read their lips. They said you *might* marry because you weren't those things."

Faith's words held Philippa motionless. The unspoken, but clear dream that Philippa would again one day marry. To speak the truth was unthinkable. It would shatter her daughter's innocence and, having had her own dreams destroyed by life early on, she would never be that person.

Her other daughter, one-year-old Violet, babbled happily while Philippa desperately fought through years of pain and bitterness to give her daughters every fanciful, hopeful word young girls were deserving of.

"Mama?" The hushed worry in that inquiry snapped Philippa to the moment.

"Mama. Mama. Mama." Violet bounced up and down, clapping her hands.

And Philippa did what any protective mama would do. "I expect any woman, regardless of age, can be a princess," she lied. Time had proven that the very tales she read to her daughters, the same ones she herself had devoured as a child, were as real as magical mirrors and talking animals.

"Do widows marry again?"

Philippa snuggled Violet. "Some do." The foolish ones. The desperate ones. And after marriage to Calvin, she was no longer a naïve fool. With the funds he'd left her, she certainly was not desperate.

"And what of you?" Faith surged upright and layered her palms atop Philippa's knees. "Will you have a happily ever after?"

Coward that she'd always been, Philippa looked to the nursemaid, who took her unspoken cue. Rushing over, the pretty young woman held her arms out for Violet. Philippa kissed the baby's plump cheek and handed her youngest daughter to Miss Cynthia. "I already have my happily ever after," Philippa said softly, ruffling the top of Faith's dark curls. "I have you and Violet and I will never need anyone more."

Instead of her child's comfort in that assurance, Faith frowned. "But you must have a prince. All princesses need princes. Unless it is because you are a widow?" She scrunched up her mouth. "Except you are not one of those old ones like Grandmother said. So surely you might marry."

Philippa had been married. She'd rather dance through the fiery flames of hell than make another wedding march. Forcing a smile for Faith's benefit, Philippa dropped another kiss atop her head. "It's time to see to your lessons."

With her daughter's groans of protest trailing behind her, Philippa hurriedly took her leave of the nursery. Once outside and free of the quizzing, her shoulders sagged. Each time she read those fanciful tales of love and dreams coming true, the questions came all the more.

More than half-fearing Faith would follow her into the hall and put countless more inquiries to her about her marital state, Philippa quickly sought out her chambers. Closing the door behind her, she made her way over to the vanity and studied herself. The words Faith had overheard Mother and Lady Martindale speaking echoed around Philippa's mind.

Yes, the world held varying views on who and how a widow should be.

At a mere five years past twenty, Philippa was decidedly *not* old, nor gray, and most definitely not plump. Nay, she hardly fit with Lady Martindale's societal expectations of a widow. Her gaze snagged on the black widow's weeds she still wore that hung on her too-slender frame. The midnight taffeta was assuredly the most visible indication that she was, in fact, a widow.

The door opened and she spun around, her skirts snapping at her ankles. Her younger sister, Chloe, hovered at the entrance, gripping the edge of the oak panel. "Hello," Chloe's hesitant greeting carried over to her. "Hello." Yes, because when a young lady found herself widowed, with two young children no less, and moved back into her former residence, no one knew what to do, or how to be, or what to say. Not even her usually loquacious and spirited sister—the very same sister who now stood half-concealed behind the door.

Long ago, Philippa had learned to be suspicious of her sister's unexpected appearances. A schemer and meddler, Chloe's motives always portended more. Secretly, Philippa, as the daughter who'd only ever been proper, enjoyed trying to determine just what Chloe was up to. She motioned Chloe in.

With that invitation, Chloe rushed inside and closed the door behind her. "I would like to take you shopping," she said without preamble.

That is why she was here? How very peculiarly un-Chloe-like…and more than a bit disappointing for it. "I do not require anything." And she didn't. While Calvin had provided nothing in the way of a loving union, his expert handling of his estates and finances had seen her well cared for in his death. Plus, her dowry had reverted back to her. No, there was hardly a shortage of wealth. And most importantly, with his death, Calvin had given Philippa her freedom. Never again would she worry after being nothing more than a nobleman's property to get his precious heir upon. Now, she could allow her daughters a life free from their late father's constant recriminations. She could now offer her daughters the opportunity to find happiness in the world around them.

"It is not my intent to tell you how long to grieve," Chloe continued. Philippa sighed. *So this is what brought Chloe 'round.* "But it is time to step outdoors again."

Of course, it was inevitable. The expectation that Philippa would rejoin the living—or rather living, as *they* saw it. Not how she might view things, in this new reality. Annoyance needled in her belly. "I do go outdoors." To give her fingers something to do, Philippa grabbed her embroidery frame and sailed over to her bed. Feeling her sister's gaze on her, she sank onto the edge of the mattress and looked up.

Chloe's eyes were rounded saucers in her face. Was it a surprise that ever-obedient Philippa would ever dare to do something as outrageous as challenge another's opinions? "This is not about going into Jane's gardens. It is about finding your smile."

Philippa wrinkled her nose. Chloe spoke as though there was something wrong in choosing to spend the better part of her days in the gardens with her daughters for company. "I smile," she said softly. Every day her daughters, Violet and Faith, brought her more joy than she knew a heart was capable of.

Chloe gave her a meaningful look. "Surely you do not wish to remain closeted away?"

Actually, she did. Very much so. Knowing that admission would only result in further probing, Philippa did as she so often did—she remained silent. It was far easier than letting Chloe, or anyone, into the world she kept hidden—the world where she had suffered through the misery of a cruel marriage. What would revealing the truth about her marriage bring other than pain to the family she loved, a family who'd already known too much pain at the abusive, late marquess' hands? "I am quite content with my situation. Furthermore," she said, stiffening her spine. "It is perfectly reasonable for a widow to be out of Society for a year."

"Oh, Philippa," her sister murmured once more. *Oh, Philippa.* A wholly useless expression that conveyed nothing and everything at the same time.

"I do not want your pity," she said tightly.

"You misunderstand, Philippa. I am sorry for your pain."

Philippa stiffened. *I am sorry.* Or *my deepest regrets.* Those were the other familiar words given since her husband's passing. Wanting to protect her family from the truth of the pain she'd lived with, Philippa had not let anyone into her world. Not Mother. Not Alex. Not Chloe. Certainly not her brother, Gabriel, the Marquess of Waverly, who'd introduced Philippa to her husband. On most days, she was torn between hating her brother for coordinating that union and herself for allowing him to. After all, it was ultimately she who'd agreed to the match with Calvin.

Just like her family, she, too, had been content to see what was on the surface; a staid, polite, respectable man. She, weak, pathetic Philippa, had been so fixed on how reserved he was. So very different from her explosive, now dead, sire that she'd failed to notice the falsity in Calvin's smile. As such, she had never predicted that Calvin's *kindness* would be blotted out by his ruthless need for an heir.

What would they say if they knew the real truth? At the protracted silence, she cleared her throat and pulled the needle through.

Chloe moved over in a soft whir of skirts and sank to a knee alongside Philippa. "I do hate seeing you like this."

"I'm sorry," Philippa replied automatically. Often, those words came, rote, born of a child who'd been constantly making apologies to their monster of a father.

Chloe covered Philippa's fingers with her own in a reassuring caress. "You do not need to be sorry for missing your husband," she said gently.

In this moment, with her sister's aching hurt for her a tangible force, Philippa *was* sorry. It was hardly fair to accept sympathies for a loss she did not feel.

"It has been a year," Chloe said gently...needlessly.

Philippa managed a nod. Three hundred and sixty-five days of black widow's weeds. She could wear whatever Society dictated, but she could not mourn the moment a husband such as Calvin Gage went on to the hereafter. Cold. Unfeeling. Despising of his daughter with her partial deafness. Singularly driven in his quest for a male heir, there had been little redeeming in him as a husband. "I will reenter Society at my own time. When *I* am ready." She underscored those latter words with an unwavering resolve.

"Well, whether you're ready or not, you don't have much choice in the matter. Mother is expecting you to reenter Society." Just like that, Chloe yanked the earth out from under Philippa's feet.

No!

"Yes," Chloe said softly.

Had she spoken aloud? Chloe gave a wry smile, so much more in character with who she commonly was, that had their mother's intentions for them not been breathed to life, then Philippa would have found solace. But Chloe *had* said it. And now, as her sister proceeded in a very Chloe-like, practical argument on all the reasons Philippa should enter *ton* life, her mind whirred, spinning out of control. She drew her arms close and hugged the embroidery frame to her chest. She'd been married. For six years. At five and twenty years she was no fresh debutante expected to make a match, and yet, is that what her mother hoped, nay, expected of her? Panic licked at the edge of her senses. Or mayhap Jane and Gabriel didn't wish her underfoot. Her breath came hard and fast. Of course she could retire to the country alone with her daughters—

"Nor do I think it is a bad idea for you to leave this townhouse," her sister was saying, yanking Philippa back from the brink.

She blinked rapidly. "I…" *Can't*, "…will think on it."

Her sister's lips turned down ever so slightly. "Promise me you'll at least go shopping."

How desperate Chloe was to send her out. Philippa would rather sit through a lecture on propriety from their always-proper mother than visit Bond Street. No one knew that. Not her younger sister. Not her mother. And certainly not her two elder brothers. They'd always seen a proper lady who enjoyed ladylike ventures: embroidering, shopping, sketching colorful blooms, but never anything more interesting. Then, no one truly knew all the secrets she carried. Or the hopes. Or rather, the hopes she'd once carried, to laugh with abandon and speak her mind. Another pang struck her heart.

"Then Hyde Park," Chloe persisted with an unwavering resolve that would have impressed any military general. Then, Chloe gave her a long look. "Mother wishes us to join her for tea later this morn."

Tea? Philippa furrowed her brow and tried to follow that abrupt shift in discourse. "What—?"

Chloe cleared her throat in a purposeful way. "She'll be joined by Lady Audley." She paused. "Lord Matthew's mother."

That name should mean something and yet it didn't. Philippa had been so removed in the country with her husband for six years and then a six-month bereavement after his death, there had been little need or want to know any names. Particularly of gentlemen.

"He is recently widowed." Warning bells went off. Surely not. Surely after having already done her Societal duty of properly wedding she'd not be expected to… With an exasperated sigh, Chloe threw up her hands. "Lady Audley is coming," Chloe continued.

Oh, Saints on Sunday. *This* is why Chloe was here. Not because she was attempting to thrust her into Polite Society or matchmake her with another gentleman. Her stomach muscles clenched reflexively. Now it made sense.

Philippa's sister leaned close and dropped her voice to a conspiratorial whisper. "I recommend you visit the park, and…" She gestured to her elder sister's black taffeta skirts. "If you wish to silence Mother on another matter, I'd at least don gray." With a wink, Chloe hopped to her feet and rang for Philippa's maid.

Philippa had never been so grateful for her younger sister's loyalty. How much braver and stronger Chloe had always been. She'd long been a master at sidestepping their mother's plans for her. *Where I've long stayed indoors, afraid to embrace life.* "Thank you," she said softly and set down her embroidery frame.

A moment later, the door opened and Philippa's maid, Ella, stepped inside.

Chloe gave a wave of her hand. "Do not give it another thought." She swept to the front of the room and then with her hand on the door handle, paused. "What you must give another thought to, are Mother's intentions for you."

Philippa balled her hands into the fabric of her skirt. As a girl, she'd never been a match for her mother and Gabriel's goals for her. They saw in her a young debutante who could make an advantageous match with a respectable, honorable gentleman. She bit her lip hard. That is all he'd ever been to her family—respectable, honorable Calvin. And secretly, in a shameful way that would have shocked all, she'd resented that not a single member of her family had seen Calvin for the monster he'd been. Yes, the Edgerton patriarch had been a merciless devil who'd beat his children. But there were other forms of cruelty…and not a single one of her siblings had looked enough to see that.

Hands settled on her shoulders and she jumped as Chloe, of like height, met her gaze squarely. "They expect you to eventually wed," she said quietly. "Because that is always the expectation, isn't it? But you've been married, Philippa." Yes, she had. For six years. Unable to meet her sister's eyes, she slid her gaze beyond Chloe's shoulder. "Do you know," her sister murmured more to herself. "For so many years, I believed yours was nothing but a formal arrangement made with Gabriel's influence. A passionless man he attended school with whom Gabriel respected for being just as staid as he was." Philippa went still. Chloe lightly squeezed her shoulders. "I have seen you this year, and your mourning, and realize how wrong I've been. You loved him." The words were spoken more statement than anything else and Philippa's throat worked. "And regardless of what Mother wishes, I'd not see you wed any man, as you've already known love." She paused. "Unless you wish to, that is."

Philippa bit the inside of her cheek. Chloe expected something. An affirmation? A "thank you"? What was it? For a brief moment, Philippa could not see past the always-present bitterness that threatened to consume her. "There will never be another," her voice shook with the force of that truth.

"You are certain," Chloe pressed. With her determination she'd make a better matchmaker than their mother and Gabriel combined.

Alas, there would have to be others Chloe maneuvered into marriage. "My husband is dead," Philippa said with a solemnity that dimmed the mischievous sparkle in her sister's eye. She managed a smile, grateful as her maid approached with a silver satin dress. Desperate to be free of her sister's probing stare and words, she set her a task. "Will you see the nursemaid has the girls readied?"

"Of course," Chloe said. She opened her mouth. *Please do not say anything else on my husband.* And perhaps, their thoughts had moved in some kind of harmony, for Chloe left.

As soon as the door closed, Philippa's shoulders sagged. Where she was concerned, her sister saw precisely what Philippa had allowed her to see. Broken-hearted, widowed-too-soon wife. And as her maid helped her change out of her long-worn widow's weeds, guilt stabbed at her for perpetuating a lie.

Just as Lady Martindale did, the world had expectations of a widow. And Philippa had played her part. Just as she'd done since Calvin drew his last breath. Yes, she'd convinced even her family that she was a woman desperately grieving the loss of her husband. But the truth was, ever since Calvin's death, she'd never felt more alive. And she certainly wasn't sad.

Not even a little bit.

CHAPTER 2

$\mathcal{M}$ILES $\mathcal{B}$ROOKFIELD, THE $\mathcal{M}$ARQUESS OF Guilford, preferred riding in Hyde Park during the early morn and this nine o'clock hour belonged to him. There was no nagging mother worrying about her four marriage-aged, unwedded children. There were no marriage-minded young ladies *seeking* his attentions. There were no headaches or hassles that came from being forced to make insignificant greetings to other lords just for the sake of propriety.

What there was on this particular day was a child in the middle of the path. Peering down the gravel riding trail, Miles drew on the reins of his mount, Whisper, and brought the chestnut to a quick halt. *Of all the blasted… How had a child come to be alone in the middle of Hyde Park?*

Particularly such a small child. It looked practically a babe to him, but as a bachelor still at almost thirty years of age, the whole details of those tiny persons were really beyond him. Furrowing his brow, Miles skimmed his gaze over the horizon, looking for the attending nursemaid. But for the morning birds taking flight over-head, the landscape remained empty. With a click of his tongue, he nudged his mount into a slight trot. Careful to not startle the child by riding up quickly on her, Miles brought Whisper to a stop and swung his leg over his mount. He swiftly looped the horse's reins about a nearby elm and started over. "Hello," he called out as he strode forward.

Kneeling on the side of the riding path, a girl with tight, dark ringlets and dressed in a fine white frock remained with her head bent, while gathering yellow buttercups from the edge of the graveled trail. A small book lay discarded at her side. By the quality of her satin skirts, she belonged to a respectable family. His frown deepened and he glanced around once more. What manner of nursemaid lost her charge? And what in blazes was he to do with a lost child?

Miles stopped beside the girl and she glanced up. "Hullo." She smiled and returned her attention to the small flowers.

Doffing his hat, he beat it against his leg. Why in blazes could he not have brought Bainbridge with him? In addition to being his only friend in the world, Jasper Waincourt, the Duke of Bainbridge, had the distinction of being a father and he'd *certainly* know a good deal better how to be with a lost, peculiarly silent girl. He looked around again, hopeful that reinforcements were on the way—surely, someone had to be looking for the child. All he had to do was wait for them to arrive. When no much-needed nursemaid or mama came rushing forward, he dropped awkwardly to his haunches. "Uh—do you have a mother?" he asked and then grimaced. Of course she had a mother. The *better* question being, was whether that negligent parent or servant were about. "Or, rather, do you have a mother, here?" he amended.

The little girl hummed a discordant tune and tipped her head back and forth in time to her off-tempo song.

Miles shoved to his feet. At an absolute loss, he beat his hat hard against his leg in tune to her singing. *Now, what?* His last dealings with children had been two decades earlier when he'd been ten and the last of his siblings had been born. Since then, beyond the Duke of Bainbridge's two small children, he'd no interaction with those little humans.

Even with his limited experience, he readily saw the folly in picking wildflowers alone, in the middle of a riding path. Moving in front of the girl, Miles again fell to his haunches.

The little girl paused and looked up. Surprise shone in her cornflower blue eyes. "You again," she blurted.

Despite the peculiarity of finding an unattended child, Miles grinned. "Me, again." He nodded to the flowers gathered in her hand. "They are pretty."

"Would you like to pick some with me?"

Miles tugged at his cravat. He'd wanted to ride his horse, which, of course, in the midst of a nearly empty Hyde Park would have been vastly more uncomplicated than picking flowers with a lost child. Nonetheless, he sank to a knee, and proceeded to pick—

Incorrectly. "Not like that," she chided. The little girl swatted at his fingers and the ghost of a smile pulled at his lips. "Like this," she said, proceeding to demonstrate. "You have to pick the stem." She lifted her head up and gave him a look.

Something was required of him. What was it? "Uh—"

"For the *flowwwers*," she said with an eye roll and by the faint exaggeration of that single word, she'd found his flower-picking skillset wanting. Then, she narrowed her eyes and gave him a frown. "Don't you give your mama flowers?"

The only thing his mother desired from him was a suitable match with Miss Sybil Cunning. "I have given my mother flowers," he settled for. Years and years ago when he'd been a small boy. He grasped at what she'd said. "And I take it these are for *your* mother?" Her absent mother. Then, given the cold ways of the *ton* mothers, they generally didn't accompany their offspring on outings to the park.

"Yes. To make her smile," she explained.

Something tugged at that thoughtful spirit. "Well, I expect they should do just that," he said solemnly. "Perhaps you might bring them to her." He paused. "Now."

The nameless child blinked and glanced about. Her eyes widened, giving her the appearance of a frightened owl. Her lower lip trembled. It was then he had confirmation of something he'd suspected from down the riding trail. "Where is my mama?"

Blast. Well, there was no avoiding it now. Forcing a smile, Miles straightened and held out a hand. "I expect we should be off to find her."

She hesitated, grabbed her book, and then placed her spare hand in his. The other clung tightly to the buttercups she'd gathered.

"Do you have a name?"

The little girl giggled. "Yes."

Miles' lips twitched. How very literal a child was; incapable of artifice that drove the world she'd eventually grow into.

"Do you?" she asked.

He paused and dropped a deep bow. "Miles Brookfield, the Marquess of Guilford. And what is your name, then?" he asked. While guiding her down the path, he worked his gaze over the grounds.

Another little giggle escaped the girl's lips.

"My name is—"

"Faith!" A cry sounded in the distance and startled the wrens from the branches of a nearby elm. The birds took off into sudden flight.

Miles peered ahead, to where a woman sprinted down the riding path tripping and stumbling over herself. She skidded to a stop before them, landing hard on her knees. She dragged the girl into her arms and knocked his hand free of the child's. The book slipped from her fingers. "Faith," she said between her panicky, raspy breaths. The fine quality of her gray satin skirts was not the type befitting a maid.

The mother. The midnight tresses and like cornflower blue eyes hinted at the familial connection.

"Where did you go?" the lady entreated.

"I was picking flowers," the child's words came muffled against her mother's chest.

The young woman drew back, searching a frantic gaze over the small figure. "Do not wander away from me or Miss Cynthia," she demanded. "Ever." The stern rebuke underscoring that utterance set the girl's lip atremble.

An interloper on the reunion, Miles shifted his weight back and forth...when the lady looked up. The panicked terror receded from her gaze, as she blinked up at him. She blinked again. And once more. "Hullo," she said hurriedly and scrambled to her feet.

Miles sketched a bow. He opened his mouth to speak when the little girl piped in.

"Mama, this is Miles. He picked flowers for you."

He blinked and followed the ladies' gazes to the wilting bouquet in his hand. Gifts between a lord and lady were forbidden. Even more so between a gentleman and a married woman.

Color blossomed on the nameless lady's cheeks. "It is impolite to refer to a gentleman by his given name," her mother murmured.

"Miles Brookfield, the Marquess of Guilford," he supplied and turned over the yellow buttercups. Surely improprieties could be forgiven for the benefit of a child's happiness?

The lady hesitated, darting her wary gaze about. Did she worry about the possible scandal should a passerby observe her receiving an offering from a gentleman?

Her daughter tugged her hand. "Mama, you are being rude. He picked them for you."

The young woman lifted her eyes once more to his. The soft blue irises momentarily froze him. When he'd been a small boy in the Sussex countryside, so many summer days he'd lay on his back staring up at the vibrant blue skies overhead. Her gaze harkened to summer skies and soft pale waters. "Thank you," she murmured, jerking him back from that lapse into madness. As she accepted the blooms, their fingers brushed and even through the leather of his gloves, the heat of her naked fingers penetrated the fabric.

Bloody hell. Miles let his arm fall to his side. He'd never been one of those roguish sorts to lust after or bed another man's wife. He glanced down at her wide-eyed daughter, staring up at him, and he forced a smile. "I cannot fully take credit for the offering, my lady. I had a most excellent tutor." The child giggled at the praise. "Thank you for the lesson on how to properly gather flowers, my lady," he said. Faith beamed and a radiant smile spread across her face. She was very much her mother's daughter. Clearing his throat, he again turned his attention to the midnight-curled mama. "I bid you good day, madam," he murmured and turned to go.

"Wait." Her softly spoken request brought him around. She held her palms up. "I did not properly thank you for helping my daughter."

"There is no need to thank me…" For some inexplicable reason that defied propriety, he needed to know the lady's identity.

The young woman sank into a flawless curtsy. "Philippa Gage, Countess of Winston," she murmured.

Lady Winston. He scoured his memory for remembrance of the lady or her husband. With her midnight curls and full lips, he'd recall a woman with a beauty to rival Aphrodite. Yet, he could not drag forth a single memory of seeing the lady in any London Season. Stooping, Miles retrieved the small leather book at the lady's feet and handed it over to her. Their fingers again brushed and a rush of charged heat went through him. Her breath caught on an audible intake. Did she too feel that warmth? Drawing his hand away, he placed his hat on once more and touched the brim. "It is a pleasure, my lady." He should leave. But he hesitated, something kept his feet frozen.

Lady Winston held his stare; high-color in her cheeks.

"Come along, Mama," her daughter urged, giving the lady another tug. That movement propelled the woman into motion and with another perfectly executed curtsy, she turned on her heel and left.

Miles remained standing, staring after them, studying mother and daughter. The lady hovered a hand on Faith's shoulder and spoke animatedly to the girl. Periodically, the child would nod. Then, the lady shot a glance back and their gazes collided once more.

A surge of awareness raced through him; an unexplainable, forbidden hungering to know more about her. Only when mother and daughter disappeared down a walking trail did it begin to subside. Giving his head a bemused shake, Miles beat a path back toward his mount. For the better part of ten years, his determined mother had been trying to match him off to a respectable young lady. He'd had little urgency to make one of those matches, because, well, there hadn't really been a pressing need. Of course he would ultimately fulfill his obligations as the marquess, but even if he did not, there was still his younger brother, who'd admirably assume the role should something happen to him. In the time since he'd left university, his friend, the Duke of Bainbridge, had been married twice, suffered the loss of a babe, remarried, and fathered two children. Yet, oddly enough, he'd not given thought of himself as a husband. Or a father…beyond the obligatory end of his role as marquess.

Thrusting aside thoughts of the young woman and her daughter, Miles reached the spot where his horse lazily munched on the grass and released his reins. Climbing astride, he nudged Whisper around and guided him in the opposite direction. Finding a lost child and her hauntingly beautiful mother was certainly enough excitement for the—

A sharp cry rang out. Heart hammering, Miles jerked on the reins. Wheeling his mount around once more, he set out after the nearby call of distress.

CHAPTER 3

Philippa WAS SENSIBLE. SHE'D LONG been practical and proper and demure. It was those traits that had snared the notice of her late husband and led to a predictable courtship and subsequent marriage.

Yes, she was hardly the manner of woman to note a towering, ginger-haired gentleman with exquisitely sculpted features. And *certainly* not the manner of woman who allowed herself to steal a glance back for a final glimpse of said gentleman's perfect figure. Except, he had rescued her wandering daughter…and picked flowers with her, and surely a gentleman such as that warranted a lingering look.

Such intrigue was dubiously rewarded. She glanced back and promptly stumbled. With a gasp, she fell sideways, coming down hard on her hip. Her daughter's soft cry cut across her distracted musings of Lord Guilford. "Mama!"

What in blazes had she stepped in? Philippa looked to her foot, partially dangling inside a rabbit hole. Bloody rabbit hole. The fairytale book she'd brought to read to her daughters lay mockingly beside it. She really *should* have been attending where she was walking.

"Oh, Mama. You *arrre* hurt." Worry stretched out that syllable.

As she removed her foot from the hole, pain radiated from her ankle and she moved it in a slow, experimental circle. "Not at all," she assured. Seated on her buttocks, with her skirts rucked about her ankles, she managed a smile. It was nothing other than her pride now smarting. It was fitting that she was now so inelegantly sprawled in the trail after being so gauche and clumsy in staring after a gentleman who'd been kind to Faith. Philippa made to stand, when Cynthia's sharp cry cut across the horizon.

The young nursemaid rushed over, shifting Violet in her arms. "Oh, my lady," she cried, with a fervor more suited to a carriage accident than a little stumble in the park.

She sighed. Then, she'd always been weak, pathetic Philippa, doing exactly as people wished to keep everyone *happy*. Doted on by all. "I assure you, I am fine," she murmured and once more made to stand, when thundering hooves sounded in the distance.

They looked as one. Philippa's heart did a funny leap. He'd returned.

The Marquess of Guilford brought his mount to a stop. In one fluid movement, he dismounted, tethered his towering horse to a nearby oak, and strode toward their quartet. He dropped to a knee beside Philippa. "Are you hurt, my lady?" he asked, in a mellifluous baritone that caused her heart to speed up another beat.

Unable to drag forth words, Philippa shook her head and then glanced at her ankles. She gasped and rushed to cover her exposed lower legs.

"My mama is hurt," Faith said, when Philippa failed to respond.

The marquess shifted his gaze from her feet and she braced for his questioning. Instead, he moved his attention to the little informant. "Is she, my lady?" he asked in gentle tones.

"Oh, yes. She stepped in a rabbit hole because she was not looking where she was going."

As her daughter proceeded to chatter like a magpie, Philippa cocked her head. Never in the course of her life had a gentleman taken the time to speak to her as a woman, let alone a small girl. Her own father, God rot his soul, had been a dark devil who'd beat his daughters with the same frequency he'd beaten his sons. As a woman, her elder brothers had taken little interest in her future or her happiness, beyond the proper, formal match coordinated by her eldest brother. And yet, here was this man…a stranger, speaking to her child as though she were an equal, when gentlemen tended to not see a child, and most especially not a female one.

"Isn't that right, Mama?"

Blinking wildly, Philippa looked from her daughter to the nurse-maid cradling Violet, and then to the marquess. Each stared at her, expecting something. Her mind raced. Just as Philippa was not the manner of woman to not attend where she was walking or to stare after a gentleman, neither was she the one who woolgathered while others spoke. She attended conversations. She worried her lower lip. Or she did. Normally. Not now. And when possessed of an absolute lack of idea on how to respond, she opted for the very safe, "It is."

A lazy smile turned the marquess' lips up and her maid gasped.

Philippa's stomach dipped and she realized she'd said the absolute worst thing.

"See, my lord," Faith said loudly, beaming. "I told you my mother was looking back at you. That is why…" Philippa choked on her swallow. "She stepped in the hole."

Mortification set her cheeks ablaze. "I was… I was…" *Please let that rabbit hole widen and suck me under…*

His smile deepened, revealing two even rows of gleaming white teeth. No gentleman had a place being so wholly beautiful…*even his teeth.* "Allow me to check your ankle for injury, my lady," he murmured.

And when presented with the option of debating whether or not she'd been staring curiously after him, or having him probe her decidedly uninjured ankle, Philippa gave a small nod.

The marquess slightly lifted her satin skirts and, with infinite tenderness, removed her boot. Her breath caught. Head bent over her ankle and the early morning sun shining off his ginger-blond strands, Lord Guilford gently pressed and probed the sensitive flesh; his touch burning her like the hot summer sun.

This is scandalous. I am in the middle of Hyde Park with a stranger, whose hands are on my person…

And never in the course of her life had she ever dared anything that was remotely scandalous. Perhaps if she had, she'd not have ended up married to the cold, soulless man she had. As such, she bit hard on her lower lip, while this gentleman trailed his fingertips over the curves and arches of her ankle and foot; his touch rousing delicious warmth that set off a wild fluttering in her belly.

He lifted his gaze and their stares collided. A spark of passion lit his eyes, reflecting the same current running through her. There should be the appropriate modicum of embarrassment at being caught watching him. And yet…she fixed on his face. She, who'd always demurely looked away and certainly never did something as bold as meet a gentleman's eyes.

"Is my mama all right?" Faith's concerned tone slashed across the charged moment and Lord Guilford promptly lowered her skirts.

"I believe she is," he said, reassuringly. The marquess stood, his midnight cloak whipping about him. "If you'll lead Her Ladyship's children to their carriage," he instructed the maid and in one fluid movement, bent and swept Philippa into his arms. Heat singed through the fabric of her satin dress as he drew her against the powerful wall of his broad chest.

She gasped. "What…?"

He looked down at her and quirked a ginger brow. "Surely you do not expect I can leave you laying in the middle of Hyde Park, my lady?" he drawled with a sardonic twist to those words.

God help her. If she were at all honorable and proper she'd insist there was no injury. She would correctly inform him that she was, indeed, fine to walk. "Thank you," she breathed.

He flashed another one of those smiles that sent her heart tripping into double time. "It is my pleasure," he said, as he strode towards the carriage.

Gentlemen were not supposed to be these six-foot three-inch towering, muscular figures. They were supposed to all be like her heavily-padded, more than slightly soft late husband. Her fingers curled reflexively about the marquess' powerful bicep. Philippa's pulse raced. After all these years of indifference to her husband, she'd believed herself incapable of the heady desire that sent her thoughts into riot. Now that myth was shattered in Hyde Park, in the arms of a stranger, no less.

As they made their way in silence, the occasional passersby stared with open curiosity and Philippa burrowed closer into Lord Guilford's arms. The scent of sandalwood, so wholly masculine, and not those fragrant florals preferred by her late husband wafted around her senses, blissfully distracting. She closed her eyes and ignored those curious stares that portended gossip. There would come time for Edgerton disapproval later. For now, there was this ginger-haired gentleman who so effortlessly carried her through the grounds.

"I confess," the marquess began, bringing her eyes flying open. "I know that we must have met before, my lady, but to my shame, I cannot bring forth a memory."

Bitterness twisted in her belly; harsh, ugly and real. "Since I made my Come Out seven years earlier, I have spent the majority of my time in the country," she said softly. Six of those years where she'd been treated as nothing more than a broodmare her late husband had gotten child after child upon. Children who had never mattered to Calvin. But to Philippa, even with her loathing for her husband, those babes had been precious souls in her pregnancies. She'd journeyed through hell with them, only to emerge solitary at the end of their battle—left with nothing but a husband who was angry for all the wrong reasons. All the well-hidden hatred for her late husband boiled to the surface, scaring her with its power.

Lord Guilford paused and looked down, their gazes meeting. The heated intensity of his green-eyed stare shot through her; eyes that could see into a person's soul and dig forth all those darkest, most coveted secrets. "That is a shame, my lady," he said quietly.

And, of course, his words were spoken for politeness sake, but her breath hitched. "Philippa," she blurted, as he continued walking.

He again halted.

She wet her lips. "My name is Philippa. Given the circumstances of our…meeting, I expect you might call me by my given name." As soon as the indecent offer left her lips, heat scorched her body, threatening to burn her inside out. Only shameful widows went about offering strangers the use of their Christian names and she would never be one of those wanton creatures.

"Philippa," he murmured, wrapping those three syllables in his husky baritone and set off another round of fluttering in her belly. He shifted her in his arms, to touch the brim of his elegant black hat. "I am Miles."

Miles. Strong, commanding, and direct. It suited him perfectly.

Up ahead, her daughter, Faith, paused and looked over her shoulder. She waved excitedly. "Are you all right, Mama?" she called, her voice carrying on a spring breeze.

Her heart pulled at that devotion. Since she was born and Calvin had disdained her because of her gender alone, Philippa had forged a special bond with the tiny human entrusted to her care. She cupped her hands around her mouth in a move her mother would lament and called back. "I am quite all right," she assured. Faith returned her attention forward.

"She is devoted to you," the marquess...*Miles* observed quietly.

Philippa stiffened. After all, one could hardly explain to family, let alone a stranger, that they'd been so since Faith's birth when the late earl sneered down at the girl babe in her arms. "She is," she said softly. "She worries after me."

As soon as the revealing words slipped from her lips, she bit down on the inside of her cheek, wishing to call them back. Alas, they'd been uttered. She held her breath. Mayhap he'd not heard. Mayhap he'd not probe. After all, he was a stranger and gentlemen didn't truly worry after women. Not enough to *ask* those probing questions. Certainly not of a stranger.

Miles frowned. "And what does she worry about?" There was a hint of something primal and primitive in that inquiry that sent warmth spiraling to her heart. Even her brothers—Alex had seen her more of a burden he didn't care to chaperone and Gabriel as a miss to be properly married off to a man who'd never harm her—had never been protective in that sense of her as a woman.

She cleared her throat. She'd already said too much. "She wishes to see me happy." Except that reassurance only brought his ginger eyebrows dipping lower. "She wishes to see everyone happy," she hurriedly explained. It was simply the manner of child Faith was, that she asked after and worried after everyone else's happiness.

Some of the tension left Miles' shoulders.

At last, they reached the waiting carriage and the marquess effortlessly shifted her inside the conveyance. His broad, powerful frame swallowed up the expansive carriage. He paused, their gazes locked and another shock of energy passed between them. "Philippa," he said for her ears alone.

And then he ducked out of the carriage. An inexplicable rush of disappointment went through her at the loss and she gave her head a hard shake. Silly thoughts. And she was never, ever, ever silly.

Moments later, her daughters and their nursemaid occupying the opposite bench, the driver closed the door. As the elegant black barouche rocked forward, she pulled back the edge of the curtain and stared after the retreating marquess. He, in their brief, chance meeting, had shown more interest in her daughter than her late husband ever had.

CHAPTER 4

AFTER CARRYING PHILIPPA TO HER carriage, Miles returned for his mount.

The chance meeting with the lady with midnight curls, thoughts of the quiet young mother with her expressive eyes, swirled around his mind. Unwelcome thoughts. One about the lady's bow-shaped, crimson lips and trim, delicate figure. Thoughts he had no right having of her, given the lady's status as a married woman. For even as most lords took their pleasures with unhappy wives, Miles had never been that man. He'd never been a rogue or rake or deliberate charmer. Mayhap that was why ladies of the *ton* had never clamored for his notice.

As Miles gathered his reins and made to climb astride and resume his previously interrupted ride, something from the corner of his eye caught his notice. Reins in hand, he walked over to it. Faith's leather bound volume of *The Little Glass Slipper* lay forlornly forgotten beside the spot Philippa had fallen.

Miles quickly retrieved it, studying the gold lettering on the front of the tome.

Who was Lady Philippa? His own mother, devoted to her family though she was, had never done something as outrageous as gallivant through Hyde Park. And certainly she hadn't read to her children. No, there had been nursemaids and tutors to properly attend her offspring. From two exchanges alone, Philippa had shown herself to possess more unrestrained love and emotion and there was something beautiful in that unwillingness to prevaricate.

Miles tucked the small book inside his jacket.

Abandoning his hope of a distracting ride, he mounted Whisper and made for his Mayfair townhouse. As he guided his horse from the park, through the awakening streets of London, the memory of Lady Philippa's full, crimson lips tempted him. Taunted him. And he thought of all the wicked things he would do with—Miles swallowed a groan. *Enough.*

Reaching the front of his ivory stucco townhouse, Miles drew on the reins.

The dutiful servant, Gavin, came forward to collect Whisper.

"Gavin, a good day, isn't it?" he asked as his feet settled on the pavement.

"Lord Guilford," the older groom with his white, more than slightly receding hairline smiled. "You are late." Such a statement came from a man who'd long, long ago learned Miles' daily routine in London of riding early; a routine he'd not deviated from... not even during the winter months.

He grinned. "I was detained." *Thinking of another man's wife.* He made a sound of disgust. Doffing his hat, Miles took the handful of steps two at a time and sailed through the front entrance as the butler opened it. "Terry," he greeted, tossing the article to the other man who easily caught it.

"My lord."

With excited energy thrumming inside, Miles whistled and made his way through the townhouse to the breakfast room. He stepped inside and his whistling tune trailed off for a discordant, weak finish. His youngest, unmarried sister, Lettice, sat at the table, staring at him.

He caught her gaze. *Go,* she mouthed. "Er..." Miles briefly eyed the door and then wheeled around.

"Miles?"

Swallowing a sigh, he shifted his direction and made his way to the sideboard. "Yes, Mother?"

"What is the meaning of this?" she demanded, as he piled his plate with eggs, bacon, and sausage.

"My breakfast?" he drawled, not deigning to glance at his perturbed mother. "I am having—"

"Not your morning meal, Miles," she said sharply as he turned around. She gave her daughter a pointed stare and Lettice promptly surged to her feet.

He silently cursed. So it was to be one of *those* mornings. Miles stared after his quickly retreating sibling with no small degree of envy. Usually, the only thing that set their mother off on such a temper was the unwedded state of her children. The remaining three of her children, that was. Alas, one of them did reserve the majority of that displeasure.

"I asked you, what is the meaning of this news?" his mother repeated, brandishing a note at her side.

With deliberate, methodical movements, he snapped open his white linen napkin and placed it on his lap. "I daresay I've no idea what you are talking about, Mother." And he didn't. Usually, he did. But he was never one of those, nor had he ever been one of those rogues whispered about in the papers so, usually, her displeasure just had to do with his still unwed state.

"Well, I expect this from your brother. He is a shameful rogue who cannot be bothered to leave his clubs and bachelor residence. But you?" In a very unladylike display, his mother tossed the ivory vellum at him. It landed with a thump beside his plate. "You are no rogue." Yes, she was right on that score. But there had been something decidedly wonderful in holding Lady Philippa's delicate foot in his hand.

Ignoring the page, he picked up his knife and the flaky, white bread off his plate. "I am not in the mood for your games, Mother," he drawled, buttering the bread. He'd much rather think about the lovely Lady Winston with her guarded eyes. What made a woman so cautious? And why did he have this desire to know?

"Then mayhap you are in the mood for this?" she carped and brandished that same folded sheet. "It is a note from the Viscountess Lovell." He paused, mid-bite. Viscountess Lovell, one of his mother's many second cousins. The two women, both mothers to twins and also three unwed children had struck up quite the friendship over the years. Nor had either of them been discreet in their intention to see Miles wed the viscountess' oldest daughter, still unmarried at eight and twenty. In fact, an understanding of sorts had been reached between those women. "I see I have your attention now," she retorted. "What were you doing in the park with an Edgerton?"

He furrowed his brow, his mother's unexpected question throwing him off course. An Edgerton? And here he'd been thinking her displeasure stemmed from the striking beauty in the park. "What in blazes is an Edgerton?"

His mother closed her eyes and her lips moved as though in prayer. When she opened them, impatience sparked in her gaze. "The Edgerton family. The men are rogues who marry scandalous creatures. The daughters are deplorable."

He tightened his mouth. As devoted as she'd proven to her children through the years, his sole surviving parent had long put rank and respectability above all else. And given his still unwedded state at nearly thirty, he'd earned her greatest frustration. "I do not personally know the Edgerton family," he said between tight lips and motioned a servant forward. "Nor if I did, would I be in the habit of defending my connection to those people, as though I were a child." He held out his glass for the footman, who filled his glass with steaming coffee and backed away.

His mother opened and closed her mouth. "You do not know the Edgertons, then?" Suspicion laced her question.

Miles blew on the contents of his glass. "I do not."

Furrowing her brow, she reached for the paper and folded it closed. "My apologies," she said in an unexpected display of remorse. Some of the tautness left her shoulders as she sat back in her seat. "I should trust Alaina's sources are not always correct." Ever correct. "I will tell her." She let loose a relieved laugh. "Of course you'll not deviate from the pledge to marry Sybil."

The pledge. That long ago promise to his mother, he'd made years earlier that if he was unwed at thirty, he'd marry the viscountess' eldest, now spinster daughter, Miss Sybil Cunning. He shifted in his seat. Odd, with that inevitable date rapidly approaching, that long-ago pledge sent unease tripping in his belly.

"Why are you doing that?" With a renewed wariness, she leaned forward in her seat.

He stilled. "Doing what?"

She slashed her hand in his direction. "Shifting about in that manner?"

Miles dragged one hand through his hair. "I don't know what you—"

"Regardless," his mother went on. "I knew you'd not be so

insensitive to take on with the Edgertons." She let out a small, relieved laugh. "Why *would* you ever be carrying a woman through Hyde Park?" He froze. "It is preposterous. It is…" She immediately ceased her prattling. "What?" She slapped her hand over her mouth. Horror rounded her eyes. "You *did* carry a woman through the park? An Edgerton?"

He frowned. "The young lady fell. It hardly seems fair to question her respectability simply because she had the misfortune of miscalculating a rabbit hole," he amended. After all, carrying a married woman who'd been injured was vastly safer than a young, unmarried debutante. At least in his mother's eyes. Even if the lady did have a lean figure he could span with his hands. At his mother's absolute silence, Miles blew once more on his drink and then took a sip.

Then, she buried her face in her hands and groaned.

His frown deepened. "Surely, you'd not have had me leave her and her young daughters there without aid?"

She let her hands fall to the table; the frustrated, resigned glimmer in her eyes, a woman of propriety who knew that he couldn't have very well not come to the aid of a fallen stranger.

"Furthermore," he went on. "The gossips," Viscountess Lovell, that bloody shrew would be better used serving the Home Office, "were incorrect in their reporting. It was not an Edgerton, but rather Lady Winston." The lady's haunting visage flitted before his eyes. What caused the glitter of sadness in that endless blue stare? Or had he merely imagined that glimmer?

His mother stitched her eyebrows into a single line. "Lady Winston?" she parroted back.

He gave a tight nod and, setting his glass down, picked up his fork and knife.

"With her family's notorious reputation, I expect the lady, a widow," she spoke that word with the same vitriol as she might a harlot or courtesan, "has arrived in London with wholly dishonorable intentions."

Miles snapped his head up. "A widow?" The young woman, with her sad eyes and two daughters, was, in fact—

"Indeed." Mother pursed her lips. "And you were seen carrying her about Hyde Park." She tossed her hands up. "Is it a wonder the viscountess is outraged?"

"Yes, it is," he said dryly. "I would expect her to be a good deal more outraged if I'd simply left an injured lady on the ground without the benefit of help."

His mother continued as though he hadn't spoken. "Regardless, you need but demonstrate your devoted interest in Sybil by dancing two sets with her at Lady Essex' upcoming ball."

Two consecutive sets constituted an offer of marriage. Short of public ruin, it was an act that would send the loudest signal of his intentions for the lady. So why, given his promise to his mother to marry the lady by the time he reached thirty, did he hesitate? "I'm not yet thirty, Mother," he said, with deliberate humor infused into his reminder.

She swatted the air with a hand. "Oh, do not tease. You'll be thirty the day the Season ends." Three weeks. Three weeks until he made a formal offer to a lady he'd known as a child, who really would make him a fine enough wife. They'd played as children and grew somewhat distant as adults. But to their mothers, the expectation had always been there just the same—they would marry.

Surely, Sybil desired more than that. He did. Or he had. Through the years, he'd been quite content in his bachelor state, with the eventual hope that there would be…more. That there would be a lady who desired more than the title of marchioness and the wealth and prestige that came with the noble position. A woman who was content with a noble gentleman, rather than a practiced charmer. Alas, there hadn't. And a promise to his mother, given when he was a man of three and twenty, had been made. How to account for the regret that now rolled through him?

His mother rose in a flurry of skirts, bringing his attention to the moment. "If you'll excuse me, I am paying a visit to Lady Lovell." She pursed her lips. "I will take it upon myself to reassure her that nothing untoward occurred. After all, the lady was injured, correct?"

The reminder only conjured the memory and feel of Lady Philippa's foot in his hand; the satiny smoothness of her soft skin. Had he imagined the breathy sigh as he'd run his fingers over her instep?

"Miles?"

"Uh…indeed, she was." By the narrowing of her eyes, his mother was not in the least mollified. Without another word, she swept from the room, leaving him with blessed silence and the memory of the *widowed* Lady Philippa.

The woman whose book he carried in his pocket. No doubt, she'd been reading the child's tale to her daughter, Faith. And why the girl was surely missing it, even now.

Miles climbed to his feet. Yes, the *least* he could do was see it properly restored to the pair.

Except, as he took his leave, why did it feel as though his intended visit had more to do with seeing the lady than anything else?

CHAPTER 5

"MY LADY, LET ME HELP you," Mary the young maid said quickly.

Later that afternoon, servants rushed about Philippa with the same attentiveness she'd received the eight times she'd been with child. She swallowed a sigh, hating that hovering concern, preferring the privacy of her own company. Alas, to her family and servants, she'd been the weak Edgerton—the most in need of protecting, the one afraid to speak her mind. *But haven't I been? Haven't I, with my willingness to wed a gentleman whose eyes I couldn't even meet because he'd been touted as a good man, proven that very thing?* Oh, how she despised what she'd allowed life to shape her into— an empty shell of someone she was not.

"Are you certain you are all right?" Faith asked, snapping Philippa's attention sideways to the too-large King Louis XIV chair where her daughter sat swinging her legs back and forth. The girl had remained at her side for the past hour, refusing to abandon her post, to return abovestairs for her lessons.

"I am quite hale and hearty," Philippa assured her. Hale and hearty were words very rarely uttered about her, but Philippa knew how important it was that she set Faith's mind at ease. This was her daughter; a girl who'd known recent loss and Philippa would not allow uncertainty about her mother's well-being to hang over her. She leaned over and brushed her daughter's knee. "Look at me. No harm will come to me," she promised, as a maid gently lifted her ankle and propped a pillow under it as though she

were a fragile piece of china. How very determined everyone was
to see her as a frail woman in need of coddling. For years, it had
been that way. Too many years. A scream of frustration bubbled
from the surface and climbed her throat, demanding to be set free.
Philippa clamped her lips shut to keep it buried.

"Not like Father?" Her father; healthy one day and dead of an
apoplexy the next.

She leaned over and collected Faith's hand. "Look at my lips,"
she ordered loudly. Too many times, too many words were lost in
translation due to Faith's partial loss of hearing. Her daughter had
become adept at making proper sense of sentences through studying lips. Philippa waited until her daughter's attention was fixed
on her mouth. "As long as it is within my power, I will never, ever
leave," she promised. It was a promise she'd no right making; one
beyond her grasp and, yet, she'd lie to the Lord on Sunday if it
would erase fear or hurt from her children's lives. But the decision
of whether to subject herself to further pregnancies was *now* in
her power.

"You almost did." Faith's lower lip quivered. "A lot."

Yes, she had. Her fingers tightened about her daughter's hand
and she forced herself to lighten her grip. The agony of endless
birthings and inevitable losses, several early, most late, which had
left her weak from blood loss. The doctor had warned the late earl
of the perils in subjecting Philippa to any further childbirths. She
drew in a steadying breath and battled the remembered horror
cleaving away at her insides. Never again. Never would she again
risk leaving her daughters behind, all to give a lord that highly-de-
sired heir.

"But I didn't," she said, proud of the even delivery of those three
words. "And it should give you proof that I'll not go anywhere."
In those many times she'd lain weak, fighting to survive, she'd bar-
tered her soul for survival, unwilling to leave Faith alone with the
cold, emotionally deadened earl. A man who'd sneered at Faith's
partial deafness and who'd lambasted Philippa for never giving
him a boy. In those darkest days when she'd hovered between life
and death, all that had kept her alive had been her daughter.

Faith slipped off her chair and perched on the edge of the sofa
Philippa occupied. "Do you promise?" she asked, taking her mother's face between her small hands.

Philippa crossed her heart. "I promise," she murmured, battling back the ever-present maternal guilt in making a pledge she couldn't truly keep in their uncertain existence.

Frantic footsteps sounded in the hall and they looked to the entrance as the Dowager Marchioness of Waverly entered, with Chloe rushing at her heels.

"Philippa," her mother cried as she stopped beside her sofa. "What is this I heard of you falling?" She looked to the maid hovering at the opposite end of the chair. "Has the doctor been—?"

"It hardly merits a visit from the doctor," Philippa reassured in placating tones. Then, hadn't that always been her role in the Edgerton family? To be soft-spoken and constantly assuring everyone that all was well. Even when her heart was wrenching with the agony of the brutality she'd known at a vicious father's hands and her husband's relentless indifference. Because ultimately, everyone had their own demons to battle and hadn't the time to take on hers, as well. "It hardly hurts anymore." And it didn't. The ache, though present, had dimmed.

"Whatever happened?" Chloe asked, in her always-curious tones, as she propped her hip on the back of Philippa's seat.

"Mama stepped into a rabbit hole," her daughter helpfully supplied. "Because she was looking back at Miles," she added. *Unhelpfully.*

Silence resounded in the large parlor and Philippa's cheeks blazed hot. With her daughter's reduced hearing, Philippa had long believed Faith had honed other skills. One being her ability to see everything about her and, in this particular instance, she'd witnessed and now shared Philippa's improper regard of the marquess. "I was not staring *at* him," she said softly. Rather, she'd been staring *after* him. Entirely different things. Weren't they?

Of course, Mother broke the tense quiet blanketing the room. "Who is Miles?" she blurted. When no one was quick to reply, she looked between her daughters. "Who is—?"

"He is the Marquess of..." Faith wrinkled her brow. "Milford? Or was it Guilford, Mama?"

"Guilford," she said weakly. For the course of her daughter's five years, Philippa had quite celebrated in Faith's willingness and ability to freely speak. Having long had her voice quashed by a cruel father and an unkind husband, she'd appreciated the joy and beauty in Faith's garrulousness. This moment, however, was decidedly not one of those times.

"The Marquess of Guilford?" her mother parroted back.

Warming to the curious stares trained on her by her grandmother and aunt, Faith puffed her chest proudly. "He carried Mama."

Once more, silence reigned. Only this time, it came with probing, piercing stares. And the last thing Philippa wanted, needed, or desired was a probing, Edgerton inquiry.

"Who carried your mama?"

She swallowed a groan as Gabriel stepped inside the room. Blast and double blast.

"The Marquess of Guilford," Chloe supplied.

Philippa leaned forward and touched her daughter's cheek. "Faith, run abovestairs to the nursery," she urged.

Her daughter opened her mouth to protest, but Philippa gave her a lingering look that ended the request. "Very well," she said on a beleaguered sigh and skipped around the furniture. She paused in the doorway alongside Gabriel, the Marquess of Waverly.

"Uncle Gabriel," she said, dropping a proper curtsy.

"Hullo, Faith." He ruffled the top of her black curls, in a gesture so at odds with the coolly removed brother he'd been through the years. Then, the man she'd come back to live with, now married and so blissfully happy, had been transformed. Something tugged at Philippa. Something ugly and dark. Something that felt very much like envy. "Did you have a nice time at the park?"

"Oh, yes," she called up. "I picked flowers with Miles."

Which only earned Philippa further probing stares; this time from the eldest Edgerton sibling. She managed a smile. Of course, there would be questions. There always were with the Edgertons. Ironically, those same kin had failed to ask the most important questions about her hopes and dreams of a future. Faith slipped from the room and Philippa collected the until-now forgotten embroidery conveniently resting on the table beside her. To give her fingers something to do, she proceeded to drag the needle and thread through the white fabric.

"Well?" Gabriel drawled. Striding over, he claimed the seat directly across from Philippa. And just one additional probing Edgerton stare pricked her already burning skin.

"I fell," she said under her breath. At the protracted silence, she paused in her work and glanced up.

The trio of Edgertons stood, mouths agape.

"You mumbled," Chloe said with the same shock of one who'd first discovered the world was, in fact, round.

Philippa shook her head. "No." She didn't mumble or mutter. Ever. She was always proper.

"Yes," Gabriel said with a faint grin. "You did."

"He is correct," Chloe continued. "And you know, it pains me to ever admit Gabriel is correct about anything, but in this, he is." She paused. "You mumbled."

"I hardly think whether or not I mumbled merits a discussion," she said between tight lips as she dragged the needle through the frame once more. Then, what she had thought, wished, or wanted, had never truly mattered. She jabbed the tip of the needle into her thumb. She gasped, as the frame tumbled onto her lap...and was met, once more, with that damning, telling silence. Philippa stuffed her wounded digit into her mouth.

Her mother clasped her hands at her throat. "Did you...*stick* your finger?"

Given that she even now sucked on that same finger, Philippa opted not to respond.

"You never make a mistake," Chloe matter-of-factly observed.

How very wrong her sister was. She had made the very worst mistakes in her life; ones that moved beyond a silly scrap of linen with flowers embroidered upon it. She curled her toes into the arch of her feet and winced as pain shot up her injured ankle.

"I believe we were speaking about the Marquess of Guilford?" her mother encouraged, because, inevitably, all matters came 'round to unwed gentlemen.

"Were we?" she asked, picking up her small wooden frame, once again. He *could* be very happily married, or more, unhappily married, as she'd been for six miserable years. After all, what did she know about the gentleman? Except, would a gentleman who'd bothered to collect flowers with her daughter and took time to search for said child's mother be one of those nasty sorts that Lord Winston had been?

"He's unmarried," her mother offered.

Of course.

Every conversation invariably came back to that important detail about a gentleman:

Would you like sugar and milk in your tea? Lord So-and-So is married.
Do take care to not walk outside, lest you be caught in the rain. It
wouldn't do for an unmarried gentleman to see you without a care...

"It hardly matters whether the marquess is wed or not wed," she said in smooth, even tones, still attending her work. She'd no intention of marrying again. Ever. There was no need to spend the remainder of her days as nothing more than a body to give a lord his beloved heir and a spare while his female issue was forgotten. When her family still said nothing, she filled the void. "Lord Guilford was gracious enough to help me to my carriage." Carrying her as though she'd weighed nothing in his strong, powerful arms. Her breathing quickened and she prayed the three now studying her didn't note her body's telltale response. "That is all," she finished weakly.

The butler, Joseph, appeared at the front of the parlor, a silver tray in his gloved hands. He cleared his throat. "The Marquess of Guilford has arrived..." He looked to Philippa. "...to see Lady Winston."

Her lips parted and questions tumbled around her mind. He was here? What...? Why...?

At the protracted silence, the butler glanced about. And though she knew this surprising turn would only bring with it further Edgerton questions later, the oddest fluttering danced in her belly at the unexpected visit.

"You may show him in, Joseph" she said "Now, please excuse me," she ordered her family. "I have a visitor to attend to."

CHAPTER 6

As Miles was led through the Marquess of Waverly's townhouse, one thing became very apparent—he was being watched.

A small figure, a *familiar* figure, came racing down the corridor. "Miles!"

He smiled as Faith skidded to a halt before him. "My lady," he greeted, sketching a deep bow.

She giggled. "I'm not a grown lady, I'm just a girl." Nonetheless, she sank into a flawless, very mature curtsy. Had life taught the girl that maturity?

"Have you come to see my mama?" she asked with the guile only a child was capable of.

"I have," he answered, snapped out of his musings. "Though I expect you've seen she is well-cared for."

Faith gave a solemn nod. "Oh, yes." She wrinkled her nose. "She wouldn't let the doctor come and check her foot. She *says* she is fine." Yet again, images of Philippa's delicate slip of flesh in his hands, the satiny softness of her skin, burned in his memory. *I am going to hell. There is nothing else for it.* "She sent me abovestairs," the girl was saying.

He furrowed his brow.

"To the schoolroom," she said by way of explanation.

"Ah, of course." As a child, he'd chafed at being shut away in those miserable nurseries, preferring the invigorating Sussex air to the closed-in rooms every previous Marquess of Guilford had lost countless days to.

"Lessons on reading," she said with the same dejected tones of one who'd been deprived of a year's worth of dessert.

His lips twitched. With her flair for the dramatics she called forth memories of his now married sister, Rosalind. "And what does your governess have you reading that has you avoiding your lessons?"

"Lessons on propriety and decorum," she said in a high-pitched, nasal tone which, he'd wager these last three weeks of his bachelorhood, was a rendition of the nursery governess responsible for her tutoring. Then, the girl flared her eyes. "But I heard you had come for a visit and I sneaked away," she whispered and then stole a glance about.

Miles dropped to a knee and leaned close to her right ear. He spoke in a conspiratorial whisper. "I was known to avoid my own lessons," he said with a wink.

She blinked and shook her head. "What did you say?"

Miles creased his brow. "Uh…"

Color rushed to Faith's cheeks and she glanced down at the tips of her toes. "You said it against my right ear. I cannot hear out of my right ear."

A vise squeezed at his chest. She was partially deaf. Of course. *This* was why she'd failed to hear his approach at Hyde Park and the questions he'd posed. Missing just a beat, Miles angled his head and repeated his admission in her opposite ear.

The little girl widened her eyes all the more, so they formed round moons in her face. "My father said only terrible children skip their lessons. He said proper, good children attended their studies."

Her father sounded like a miserable, stodgy bore. As soon as the thought slid forward, guilt settled in. It was hardly fair to judge a man in death. "I suspect there is much to be learned in visiting the park and being outdoors, too, no?" he asked, instead.

She flashed him a gap-toothed grin. He dropped his voice to a conspiratorial whisper once again. "And also from reading enjoyable books about far off places." He fished her forgotten book from the front of his jacket and held it out.

A small cry escaped the girl. "My book." She hurled herself into his arms and he staggered back. "I forgot that I forgot it. And it is one of my favorites. It is about a princess and prince."

Warmth filled his chest at that absolute lack of artifice. Aware of the ancient butler staring, Miles set the girl away. "Off you go with your fairytale then," he said with a wink.

Faith waved and, turning on her heel, skipped off. He stared after her a moment and then fell into step behind the aged servant. At last, the man brought them to a stop outside an open door and Miles did a quick search of the room; his gaze landed on the delicate, slender lady stretched out on the sofa. Even with the distance between them, her eyes sparkled with some emotion—emotion he could not singularly identify, but desperately wanted to. "The Marquess of Guilford," the old servant announced.

"Joseph, would you see refreshments brought?" she asked.

The servant nodded and backed out of the room—leaving Miles and Philippa—alone.

"My lord," she welcomed in a soft, husky contralto that sent a bolt of lust through him. "Would you care to sit?"

Miles smiled and strode over, claiming the seat nearest her. "I thought we had agreed to move past the formalities of titles?"

"Very well," she conceded. "Miles." Her cheeks pinked, stirring intrigue with a widow who blushed like a debutante. She stole a furtive glance about. Did she fear recrimination over the use of his given name? His interest redoubled. "I did not expect you to…" She turned crimson. "That is…"

"I found a forgotten volume of *The Little Glass Slipper* and sought to return it."

"Oh." Did he imagine the lady's crestfallen expression? "That is, I meant, *thank you*. For returning it and for coming to my aid this morn."

The young widow dropped her gaze to the embroidery frame in her lap.

"I also wished to ask after you, Philippa," he said quietly.

"I am well," she said automatically.

She fiddled with the wood frame, drawing his attention to the skillfully crafted floral artwork on that white fabric. The delicate flowers, so expertly captured, demonstrated proficiency with a needle. Only… Miles took advantage of the lady's distracted movements to study her. To truly study her. The white lines pulling the corners of her mouth; the frown on her lips as she glared at that scrap. Such details shouldn't really signify. Not when he'd only come to return that child's book, which he'd since done. *Liar. You wished to see this woman before you now.* "You do not enjoy it, then?"

She jerked her head up. "Beg pardon?"

Miles hooked his ankle across his opposite knee and motioned to the scrap of fabric on her frame. "You look as though you'd singe it with your eyes if you could," he said with a smile.

Philippa followed his stare and then her perfect, bow-shaped lips formed a small moue. She blinked and drew that frame close to her chest with the same protectiveness of a mother bear defending her cub. "How...why...?"

He leaned forward and dusted the backs of his knuckles alongside the corner of her eye. "Here." The lady's breath caught. "You were frowning with your eyes when you were staring at it," he said quietly. *Drop your hand. Drop your hand because coming here and putting your hands upon her, in any way, is forbidden...*

Her lashes fluttered and Miles quickly dropped his hand to his side. By God, what madness had overtaken him?

IN THE SCHEME OF ALL that had transpired in the past handful of minutes, Philippa should very well be fixed on the marquess' brazen, if fleeting, caress.

And yet, instead, she was transfixed not by his gentle touch, but rather—his statement. *You look as though you'd singe it with your eyes if you could...*

Philippa ran her fingers over the edge of the frame. "I do not," she said softly.

Miles furrowed his brow.

"Enjoy it," she clarified. And with that admission, which went against every ladylike lesson ingrained into her from the cradle, there was no bolt of lightning or thundering from the heavens... and there was something...freeing in it. A wistful smile pulled at her lips. "Do you know you're the first to ever ask me that question?" Before he could reply, she rushed on. "Of course, you couldn't possibly know that as we've only just met. But you are. Correct, that is," she said, setting aside the frame. And for that, she thanked him. For seeing past her ladylike skill with that scrap and the well-built façade.

They shared a smile, as with his observation and her admission, a kindred bond was forged. A connection born in actually speaking *with* a person…something she'd never shared with her own husband. A thrill went through her. This was the intoxicating stuff recorded on the pages of those fanciful fairytales.

Miles glanced about the room and, for a moment, she believed he'd take his leave and restlessness stirred in her breast. Then, she'd be left here with the pitying stares and the sad glances and people who didn't know she despised needlepoint and proper curtsies and false smiles. She searched her mind, never more wishing that she'd been one of those ladies skilled in conversing with all the right words. "Do you ride often?" she asked tentatively. As he trained his eyes on her face, she cringed. *Do you ride often? That is the best that I could come up with?*

"Every morning when I am in London," he said at last.

Philippa filed that particular piece about the gentleman in her mind.

"And what of you?" He arched an eyebrow.

"Me?" She touched a hand to her chest. "I have never been proficient at riding," she admitted. Or conversing. Or being anything other than proper. Dull, proper, always-pious Philippa. She curled her hands into tight balls, never hating that truth of her character more than she did in this moment. She sighed. "I'm proficient at this," she said, lifting the embroidery frame once more. In a show her mother would have lamented, Philippa tossed her frame to the marquess who easily caught it in his large, gloved hand. "And so everyone, of course, assumes I *must* enjoy it. Why shouldn't I? I know how to draw the thread just so and how to craft an image upon it. Where is the pleasure in it, though?" she asked, the words just spilling out when they never, ever did.

"What, then?" At his quietly spoken question, she tipped her head. "What do you find pleasure in?"

"My daughters," she said with an automaticity borne of truth. In their world, ladies didn't speak about affection or emotion they carried for their children. And yet… "My daughters make me happy." She coughed into her hand.

He searched his piercing gaze over her face. "I expect they would," he said with a matter-of-factness that caused her heart to pull. There was a sincerity to those words, at odds with everything her own father and late husband had proven in terms of affection for children. "What else?"

She started. "What else?" What else made her happy? No one in the course of her life, not even her sister whom she adored, had ever put that query to her. As such, it was a question she'd not really given any thought to. Her existence was a purposeful one where she'd been a countess, in charge of a household staff, and her daughters' tutors and nursemaids. But she'd not always been that way. "I used to read fairytales," she said wistfully. Not unlike the books she read to her daughters. She'd forgotten until he'd forced her to think back to how those fanciful tales had once brought *her* happiness, as well. "My mother abhorred my reading selection. Called it drivel," she said with a remembered laugh. Philippa hadn't cared. She'd been so enthralled by the possibility of forever happiness promised on those pages that she'd braved her mother's displeasure. It was why she even now read to her girls from those same books.

"Is that why you stopped reading them?"

She blinked as Miles' quietly spoken question jerked her back to the present—and the impropriety of speaking so familiarly with a man she'd only just met. She firmed her lips into a line, willing herself to say nothing. Still, there was this inexplicable ease being around him, when she'd never even been comfortable around her own family. Philippa lifted her shoulders in a slight shrug. "One day," she'd been married just a fortnight, "I remember finishing a book and just realizing…" She let her words trail off.

"Realizing?" he urged, a sea of questions in his fathomless eyes.

"How very silly it was to believe in a land of happily-ever-afters." Such dreams didn't exist. Life in the Edgerton household had proven as much. Marriage to Lord Winston had only confirmed it. No, dreams of fairytales were reserved for innocent children unscathed by life. Or that is what she'd come to believe. Now, this man before her swooped into her life and stirred all those oldest yearnings she'd once carried. Feeling Miles' gaze on her, Philippa's face heated. She'd said entirely too much. Words she'd never even acknowledged to herself and suddenly it was too much. "If you'll excuse me," she said softly. "I must go see my daughters."

"Of course," he said politely and climbed to his feet.

And as he took his leave, the tension drained from her body, down to her feet. She'd long believed there was nothing more perilous than Lord Winston and his dogged attempt to get a male babe on her.

Now she feared she'd been wrong.

The gentle, tender Miles Brookfield's ability to stir her long buried dream of a happily-ever-after was far more dangerous.

CHAPTER 7

$\mathcal{P}$HILIPPA HAD NEVER BEEN SOMEONE who listened at keyholes. Where Chloe had slunk about the townhouse with her ear pressed to oaken panels, she had wisely continued on. Not because she'd not been remotely curious about what was discussed behind those thick doors, but rather, the terror at what would become of her if she was *discovered* at those keyholes. It had been an attempt at self-preservation.

Now, years later, she saw it as a testament to her weakness and failings. That self-awareness, however, was *not* what brought her to a stop outside her elder brother's office, the following morning. Philippa slowed her steps.

"…She is far too *young* to remain a widow, Gabriel…" At the insistence in her mother's tone, Philippa's stomach knotted.

"…She is in possession of her dowry, Mother… She does not need…" Whatever she did or did not need and their mother's response to it was lost to the thick wood. Philippa gave her head a befuddled shake. *This* was Gabriel? This man who spoke of her remaining unmarried, was so at odds with the practical, determined, matchmaking brother who'd introduced her to her late husband. "You cannot expect her to make a match with just any gentleman…" Gabriel continued, "…She loved him…"

Her lips pulled in a sad smile. This was, of course, what everyone saw. After all, it was easier to see the lie that your sister had loved her miserable excuse for a husband than to accept the role you'd played in the union…

"…She has two daughters… Lord Matthew would make her a splendid match…"

Oh, God. How could her mother, who'd subjected her own children to the abuses of a brutal husband, be so steadfast in her resolve to make matches for her children? She pressed her eyes closed. Her mother was no less determined to marry her off than when she'd been a debutante just on the market. Dread spiraled through her; it found purchase in her feet and those digits twitched with the need to take flight.

"Philippa," the gentle voice of her sister-in-law, Jane, sounded over her shoulder, ringing a gasp from her.

Philippa spun around. The blonde woman with a gentle and all-knowing smile stood with a book in her hands. Wetting her lips, she looked from the sister-in-law, who'd so graciously accepted her inside her home for these six months now, to the door where her brother and mother still carried on, discussing her fate and future.

The other woman gave her a gentle smile. She tucked the book in her hands under her arm and held out her spare hand.

Philippa hesitated. Jane tipped her head in the direction of the opposite hall. And when faced with being discovered any moment by her mother and brother, she far preferred the company of her sister-in-law with curious eyes.

She allowed the other woman to dictate the path they took through the house. Their slippered footfalls were silent in the halls as they wound their way through the house, to the…

Her stomach lurched as Jane stopped outside the library. A dull buzzing filled her ears, like so many swarming bees. How many times had she stood outside this very room, seeking refuge from her father's beatings? Of all the places he'd thought to look for his children—the gardens, the parlors, the kitchens—never had he, with his disdain of books and literature, come here. Now she sought a different refuge; the danger no less real.

"Philippa?" her sister-in-law gently prodded and she jolted into movement. Eyes averted, she walked at the sedate pace drilled into her by too-stern governesses. Jane closed the door and motioned to the nearby leather button sofa. "Please," she said softly. "Will you sit?"

Philippa hesitated and then slid onto the folds of the sofa. The leather groaned in protest. She folded her hands primly on her lap to still the tremble. In the months since Philippa had moved into the new marchioness' home, Jane had proven herself to be kind and patient. She didn't probe where every other Edgerton did. But neither did Philippa truly know her. Did Jane also want her married off? As her sister-in-law settled onto the seat beside her, dread knotted Philippa's insides.

"I wanted to be sure that you are happy here," the other woman began.

Philippa blinked. Happy here? A peculiar question that no one had ever put to her. The expectation had always been that, as a lady, she belonged wherever her husband, or father, or now elder brother was. "I am," she said at last. Because she was. At least happier than she'd been when she'd been a girl living in this very house. Unable to meet the searching expression in Jane's eyes, she looked about. Her stare landed on the book set aside by her sister-in-law. She peered absently at the title. *Thoughts on the Education of Daughters—*

"Are you familiar with Mrs. Wollstonecraft's work?"

Philippa shot her head up; her attention diverted away from the gold lettering on the small leather tome. She looked questioningly at the other woman.

"Mrs. Wollstonecraft," Jane elucidated, holding up the volume.

"I am not," she said softly.

"She was a writer and an advocate for women's rights," her sister-in-law explained, as she held the book out. Philippa hesitated. This was the type of scandalous work her mother would have forbidden and her husband would have burned. With steady fingers, she accepted the book. "I quite enjoy her work."

Philippa studied the title. *Thoughts on the education of daughters: with reflections on female conduct, in the more important duties of life.* How singularly…peculiar that her brother, who'd lamented Chloe's shows of spirit and praised Philippa's obedience to propriety and decorum, should have married a woman who read philosophical works, and whom he'd also given leave to establish a finishing school to educate women who dwelled on the fringes of Society. At the extended silence, she cleared her throat and made to hand the book back over.

"I've always admired her," Jane said, ignoring the book so that Philippa laid it on her lap. "Mrs. Wollstonecraft's father squandered the family's money. He was a violent man." Philippa stiffened. How much did Jane know of the abuse she and her siblings had suffered at the vile monster's hands? "She cared for her sisters," the woman went on. "And then she cared for herself."

Self-loathing filled her. In a world where she'd readily turned over her fate and future to a man simply because he was respectable and *kind*, there had been Mrs. Wollstonecraft who'd laid claim to her life. "Did she?" For what did that even entail? Even now, living with her brother and his family, she'd demonstrated a return to a life not wholly different than the one she'd lived.

"Yes," Jane said simply. Something gentle and, yet, at the same time commanding, in the woman's tone brought Philippa's gaze to hers once more. "Mrs. Wollstonecraft was not always that way, Philippa. She was compelled by her father to turn over all the money she would have inherited at her maturity to him. A miserable, mean cruel man."

Not unlike the way Philippa had turned her body over to a husband to use as a vehicle to beget heirs and boy babes. Her throat worked. "Some women come to believe the rules and expectations set forth by Society so strongly that they can't escape from those ingrained truths." Ever.

Jane scooted closer. "Ah," she said. "But that isn't altogether true." She pointed to the book in Philippa's tight grip. "One might have said as much about Mrs. Wollstonecraft and, yet, she went on to lay claim to her fate and her future. She found work." She paused and gave Philippa a meaningful look. "But more, she found joy in her work and in the control she had of her future."

Those words echoed around the room, penetrating Philippa's mind. Jane spoke to her. Encouraged her to see that she could be something different than the silent, obedient creature who, no doubt, would crumple under her mother's determination to see her wed. *Why does it have to be that way? Why must I marry where my heart is not engaged?* Her heart, mind, and body belonged to no one. Not anymore. Not in the ways Society saw it. "My mother wishes me to marry," she said, unable to keep bitterness from tingeing her words.

"And you do not wish that." Jane spoke as a statement of fact.

Philippa cast a look at the door and then absently fanned the pages. "They expect that I should find a proper," her lip peeled back in an involuntary sneer, "husband who will be a father to my girls and who will properly manage my finances."

"What do you expect for yourself, Philippa?"

She'd spent the whole of her five and twenty years working to be an obedient daughter, a proper debutante, a flawless wife. So much so that she'd never, not even once, thought about herself as anything beyond an extension of another—until now. Philippa stopped her distracted movements and her gaze collided with the center of the page.

...Taught from their infancy that beauty is woman's scepter, the mind shapes itself to the body, and roaming round its gilt cage, only seeks to adorn its prison...

"My mother's friend and her widower son came to visit." She smiled wryly.

"And do you wish to see this widower son?" Jane asked hesitantly.

"No, I do not." Her loudly spoken words bounced off the walls. She blinked. *I do not.* Her smile widened and with it went the bitterness, leaving in its stead a freeing purity. "Nor do I want my mother or brother's interference in my life." Well-meaning though it may be. She'd been the recipient of those well-meaning intentions and what had that attained her other than a miserable marriage? She slashed the air with her hand warming to the freedom of her thoughts. "And I certainly don't wish to guard my words and laughter. Or to be dull and bored by life." No, she didn't wish to ever be the lifeless creature she'd been. Lightness filled her chest.

Jane gave a pleased nod. "Then live for yourself and show your daughters how life can be, and should be, lived," she said.

Were the two mutually exclusive? How could a woman exist for herself while also putting her children before all? Another wave of awe struck her at the woman's fierce independence. She was a marchioness. An expecting mother. And she saw the running of a finishing school for ladies. *And I am here, listening at keyholes, worrying about gentlemen my mother wishes to pair me off with.*

Jane held her gaze squarely. "It is possible to be a mother and to still have control and power of your life. You do not lose yourself when you became a mother," she said with a gentle look. "You find new parts of yourself that teach you about your own strength and capabilities. You are not just your children, Philippa."

Yet for six years, she'd existed as nothing more than a woman whose sole purpose had been to birth babes. To her husband, she'd ceased to matter. She stared absently at the floor-length window. Mayhap, she never had. And now with Lord Winston gone, she was free to begin again. To speak and laugh and move without fear of recrimination. "Thank you," she said quietly.

Leaning forward, Jane rested her hand on Philippa's. "There is no need to thank me. You are my sister," she said simply. "If you'll excuse me?" She climbed to her feet. "I've a meeting shortly regarding the hiring of a new headmistress."

"Wait!" Philippa called out as her sister-in-law turned to go. She jumped to her feet and held out the book.

Jane held her palms up. "It is yours. Judicious books enlarge the mind and improve the heart."

Philippa started. "That is beautiful."

Gabriel's wife waggled her blonde eyebrows. "*That* is Mrs. Woll-stonecraft."

As the lady turned and took her leave, Philippa returned her attention to the book in her hands. Her mother would, of course, expect her to be present while she received her guests and any other time in her life she would have remained an obedient daughter with her hands primly folded, speaking on the weather and every other dull topic expected of a lady.

Pulling the gift given her by Jane close to her chest, Philippa started for the door.

She was going out.

CHAPTER 8

A SHORT WHILE LATER, WITH HER recently asserted literary independence, Philippa stood alongside the lake in Hyde Park, that same book lying on the blanket behind her.

There was not a soul present in Hyde Park. At least, not any nearby. She closed her eyes briefly and drew deep of the late spring air, filling her lungs with it. There was something so very thrilling in being away from the scrutiny of her family. And the questions of the gossips. And to just simply…*be*.

Stepping closer to the shore, she took in the smooth glass-like quality of the water. Even. Smooth. Placid. Not unlike herself.

Which only stirred that slow-building annoyance with the life she'd lived these past five and twenty years.

Desperate to break that perfect calm, Philippa bent, grabbed the nearest stone, and skipped it onto the surface.

Or tried to.

The rock hit the water with a loud *thunk* and promptly sank. If the Dowager Marchioness of Waverly was scandalized by Philippa's recently discovered appreciation of Mrs. Wollstonecraft's work, seeing Philippa now at Hyde Park, hurling stones into the water would send the woman into apoplexy.

Philippa glared at that smooth lake; that mocking reminder of her being the vapid creature she'd allowed herself to be molded into. She couldn't even manage to skip a proper stone.

With a growl she plucked another stone from the ground and

drew her arm back—

A deep, *familiar* baritone called from beyond her shoulder. "Have you ever skipped a stone before?"

Spinning, she shrieked and reflexively launched the stone. A horrified gasp exploded from her lips as it hit Miles squarely on his chest. "Miles," she cried, slamming her palm over her mouth. *He is here. Why is he here?* She swallowed a groan. Then… "I hit you with a rock."

Dismounting from his horse, he looped the reins around a nearby tree. "I daresay this is the first time I've ever been greeted by someone hurling rocks." Miles tugged off his gloves and gave a wry smile.

Horror filled her breast, threatening to choke her on embarrassment. "I am so sorry," she sputtered. "I was just…skipping stones." She gesticulated wildly and she, who was so guarded with words, found them flowing freely. "Or trying to. And…" What a blithering fool. She clamped her lips closed.

"I trust your ankle is well?" he asked, coming forward. A twinkle lit his eyes.

"Quite." Heat stole up her neck and stained her cheeks. "But do not tell my mother, as it will prove helpful for me to avoid certain activities."

"Then it wouldn't do for you to be discovered standing on the same ankle, lest it be reported back." He followed that conspiratorial whisper with a wink.

Just like that, all embarrassment at being caught skipping stones at the lake and failing miserably at the endeavor left her. An unadulterated laugh spilled past Philippa's lips. And how very wonderful it felt to laugh.

"Have you ever skipped them before?" he puzzled aloud.

She cocked her head and he motioned to the lake.

"It was deemed improper," she explained with another wry twist of her lips. How many years had she spent shaping herself into the dutiful daughter? And what happiness had that brought her?

"Ah, you are long overdue for a lesson then, my lady." Miles sifted through the pebbles littering the earth and tested one in his hand. "The secret is to find a flat, smooth stone." He pressed it into her gloveless palm and delicious shivers radiated from the point of contact. His touch was hotter than the late spring sun beating down on them. Her mouth dry, she curled her hand tight around the stone. Never in all her husband's quick, painful couplings had she known the thrill of heat as she did with this man's touch.

"Not too tight," he schooled, his grip firm but gentle upon her. How could he be so calm and unaffected while her heart raced at his nearness? "Like this," he explained, coaxing her fingers open. He drew her before him so they faced the lake, her back pressed to his chest. *Oh, goodness.* She closed her eyes a moment drawing in a deep, steadying breath. "Hold the stone between your thumb and forefinger with your thumb on top," he murmured against her ear. "Draw your arm like this," he coaxed, guiding her arm back, his mellifluous baritone washing over her like warmed chocolate. "As you fling it, cock your wrist back and give a flick." His breath fanned her ear. Coffee and mint. She breathed in the intoxicating scents. "And throw out and down at the same time," he whispered.

Philippa gave a flick of her wrist. The stone hopped three times before sinking under the surface. She gasped, touching her fingers to her lips. A giddy lightness filled her chest and she swiveled her gaze from that small triumph now below the lake to a grinning Miles. "I did it," she said with a breathless laugh. It was a small accomplishment. Surely an insignificant victory over the staid lifestyle she'd lived, but it felt real and magnificent and so wholly wonderful.

The smile on his lips faded and he passed solemn eyes over her face, lingering his gaze on her mouth. What was he thinking now?

Miles doffed his hat and beat it against his leg. "I should leave." Did she merely wish for the heavy regret coating that acknowledgement?

"Must you?" That question emerged frantic as he turned to go. He paused and her mind raced. Yes, the world would be shocked at her boldness in all but pleading with this gentleman to remain. Philippa claimed a spot on the blanket and motioned to the spot beside her. "That is, you are welcome to stay. If you wish."

I SHOULD LEAVE.

There were countless reasons to leave Philippa and resume his morning ride. But one, more important, reason to stay—he wished to be with her. Where his younger brother, Rhys, had acquired a reputation as a rogue with an ability to effortlessly woo a lady with lies and flattery, Miles had always been direct. Not that he required any skill to woo Philippa. He wasn't here for that purpose. *You are a bloody liar. You searched for her the moment you entered the park...*

Philippa stretched her legs out so that her heels nearly brushed the still water and turned her face up to the morning sun.

Possible notice from a passerby be damned, Miles claimed a spot beside her on the white blanket.

"It is beautiful, is it not?" There was a wistful quality to her question as she stared at the sun's rays shining from the glass-like surface of the lake.

He caressed her heart-shaped face with his gaze. "Most beautiful," he said quietly.

"I hate London," she said, not taking her eyes from the water. "When I am here, I can almost believe for a moment that I'm in the country."

How alike they were in that regard. "It is stifling," he said softly. "All the rigid expectations."

She shot her gaze to his. Surprise flared in their depths. "And the constant stares and absence of laughter," she added. Philippa picked up the leather book beside her and absently fanned the pages. "How odd," she whispered, more to herself.

He edged closer and the fragrant scent of lavender that clung to her skin wafted about his senses, heady and intoxicating. "What?" he urged, his tone hoarsened with a desire to know her secrets and the taste of her lips.

Philippa angled her head up. With their lips a mere handbreadth apart, their breaths mingled. "I never suspected a gentleman would know those same constraints."

Miles concentrated on his even breathing and her words to keep from claiming her lips under his. "There are expectations for all members of the peerage, then, isn't there?" he asked. A light breeze tugged at her chignon and a midnight strand tumbled over her brow. He captured that strand between his fingers luxuriating in the satiny softness of that tress. "Noblemen marry ladies hand-picked by their families."

She closed her eyes a moment. "Those proper, emotionless marriages meant to secure greater wealth and even greater prestige."

Miles froze, her lock still between his thumb and forefinger. Is that what her marriage had been?

Color rushed the lady's cheeks and she hastily pulled back. He let his hand fall to his side and cast a glance about. Alas, with the benefit of the small copse, they remained sheltered from possible observers. She cleared her throat and attended the book in her lap, drawing his gaze downward.

"Mrs. Wollstonecraft," he said with some surprise.

Suspicion darkened the lady's gaze. "Do you know of her?"

He offered a half-grin. "I am not unfamiliar with the Enlightened thinkers, my lady." Questions raged all the more about the young widow who, in their handful of exchanges and her readings of the controversial philosopher, had revealed so much. From her disdain of embroidering to her precise read on noble marriages.

The lady followed his stare, and then drew that volume almost protectively to her chest. "I only just...discovered her."

Miles stretched out his legs before him and that slight shift brought their thighs touching. The heat of Philippa's skin penetrated the fabric of her skirts and his breeches and scorched him. He swallowed a groan of desire. "And what are your thoughts, madam?"

She startled, her lips parting on a small moue. Did her surprise come in his knowing of the distinguished, yet controversial, philosopher? Or the question he put to her?

Not for the first time, he wondered at the man she'd been married to. One who spoke so coldly to a child about her lessons, what manner of husband would he have been?

"I quite like her," the lady said softly. She flipped through the pages of the book, landing on the front end of the tome. "Here," she insisted and spun the book around.

Miles accepted it and followed her finger to the passage. He quickly skimmed the writing. With each word read, a greater window inside the mysterious Lady Winston opened.

"...*Women are told from their infancy, and taught by the example of their mothers, that a little knowledge of human weakness, justly termed cunning, softness of temper, outward obedience, and a scrupulous attention to a puerile kind of propriety, will obtain for them the protection of man...*"

"It was the needlepoint," she whispered, bringing his focus from the page to her. "After you left, after you asked me about it, I thought of it. Truly." She gave her head a shake. "I thought of it when I've never truly considered it before. I followed in my mother's example—proper, obedient—and what did that gain m—?" Philippa bit her lip and looked out on the smooth surface of the lake, once more. A pink pelican glided to a stop on the water and dipped his head, searching under the depths.

What did that gain me?

Those unspoken words twisted his insides into knots. He forced himself to set the book aside. In Lady Philippa, the world saw a sad widow. But in listening to her, in hearing the words she did not say, Philippa spoke more than Mrs. Wollstonecraft. Miles and Philippa traveled down an intimate path of discourse that defied all those expectations they'd earlier spoken of. "What did that gain you, Philippa?" he asked quietly. And he didn't give a jot about those expectations.

Philippa again brought her knees close. She wrapped her arms loosely about them. A small, humorless smile formed on her full lips. "Not happiness," she said with a wryness that knotted his belly. He despised a world in which she should have known a hint of a misery. Preferred it when he'd taken her for a broken-hearted widow and not this wounded by life woman. "You asked what makes me happy and do you know what that is?" She posed an inquiry to him.

"What?" The question rumbled up from his chest. Whatever it was, in this moment, he would give it to her to drive back that bitter cynicism.

"Speaking to you," she said with an honesty that, given the expectations his mother had of him, should have terrified the hell out of him. Instead, her admission caused a lightness in his chest. She leaned forward and dropped her voice to a conspiratorial whisper. "My mother would be shocked if she knew I spoke to you, a stranger, so." He started. This woman who'd consumed his thoughts since their chance meeting, whom he'd wondered after and speculated on, was, in fact—a stranger. How singularly odd that he should feel he knew her so very well, still. She cast another look up. "Have I scandalized you?"

He winked. "I'm nearly thirty, with a rogue of a brother and three incorrigible sisters. I assure you, I do not shock easily."

A full, rich, husky laugh spilled past her lips, further deepening the intimacy of this stolen exchange. "I also have a sister," she said. "Chloe." She stared out at the lake, a wistful glimmer in her eyes. "She is my younger sister and, yet, since she was a girl, she's been so bold and courageous and fearless in showing her emotion and speaking her mind. And I…" Her lips pulled in a grimace and she gave her head a shake. "And I have been anything but those things."

Bringing his knees up, Miles matched Philippa's pose and trained his gaze on the same pelican that earned her notice. He picked up a small, flat stone beside the blanket and, with a flick of his hand, skipped it over the surface. It hopped once. Twice. A third time. And then sank. "Ah, but there are different kinds of bravery and boldness, Philippa. You are not your sister." She stiffened. Did she see herself as a shadow of that other woman? No. Her sister could not possibly be as refreshingly sincere and captivating as this lady. "But your eyes speak a tale of a woman of strength." She looked at him and their gazes met. "Even if you do not see it in yourself." He paused. "Which you should."

Her throat moved.

They returned their gazes to the lake before them and remained in a companionable silence.

Never had he before sat alone with a woman and spoken on anything beyond the polite discourse required of a lord and lady. Yet, for the ease in talking to her, there was also a remarkable ease in the comfortable silence between them. There was no urge on the lady's part to fill the void. Rather, there was a sincerity to their exchanges that he'd not ever known, not even with Sybil. He clenched and unclenched his jaw. What was it that an understanding he'd long accepted should now set off a violent restlessness inside.

"Do you know something, Miles?" Philippa asked, cutting across the quiet.

He looked at her.

"Today was one of the first times I realized that there are freedoms permitted me." He frowned as a dark thought slid in of Philippa becoming that jaded widow, preyed on by unscrupulous rakes, and a vicious desire to hunt down those nameless, faceless scoundrels and take them apart with his bare hands filled him. "Freedoms I'd been too cowardly to seize before," she continued over his silent tumult. The young lady squared her shoulders. "I am a widow. If I wish to speak to you in the middle of Hyde Park, then I'll do so unapologetically. There's no scandal to hurt me. I'm not some debutante trying to make a good match. In fact, I do not need to marry again." She paused, wetting her lips once more. "Unless I wish to."

Who would be the gentleman to woo her and bring her happiness? For surely, there was, at the very least, one man deserving of her. And why did a seething fury uncoil inside him like a serpent poised to strike? Another breeze stirred the air around them and sent ripples on the lake's surface. "But someone wishes you to marry, again?" He didn't realize he held his breath until she spoke.

"My mother." She gave her head a rueful shake. "And she knows the very person I should wed, too, of course."

"Ah. I understand that. On that point we are very much alike," he said. "Our mothers seem to be of like personalities." The rub of it was Sybil would make him a perfectly acceptable wife. They got on great as children and spoke with a familiar ease one did not often find with members of the opposite sex. And even as he hadn't wanted to marry Sybil, he would have been content in fulfilling the expectations of their families in marrying her—if it hadn't been for a chance meeting with Philippa.

In just a brief encounter, she'd stirred questions and curiosities. And desire.

This meeting only yielded a greater desire to know about a lady who so expertly stitched and then confessed to him her disdain for the activity. From that slight statement, and the glint in her eyes, he'd seen beyond the veneer of expected ladylike perfection to a woman with her vitality, who chafed at the strictures placed on her. The strength of her spirit intrigued him in ways he'd never been drawn to another.

CHAPTER 9

WITH MILES' PRONOUNCEMENT, QUESTIONS WHIRRED in Philippa. Did he intend to fulfill his family's wishes the way Philippa herself had with Calvin? The idea of Miles in a cold, empty union gutted her. And yet, thinking of him blissfully in love with that nameless lady brought with it a different kind of torture.

Absently, she gathered a stone. "So there *is* a certain lady?" she asked, pleased with the evenness of her tone. "Someone your family would see you marry?" Her hand shook and the rock shook in her trembling fingers. For her newfound discovery that morn of freedom of thought, this unguarded honesty was still foreign and roused terror in her belly. It went against the woman she'd been for so long; and freeing as it was, it rattled the foundation of her previously ordered world. She made to skip her rock.

"There is," he said matter-of-factly and her carefully selected stone thudded noisily in the water. A dull pressure weighted her chest. "Though there is no formal arrangement," he said solemnly, "just an expectation among two mothers." There was a guarded quality to his tone.

Were those words for her benefit? Her heart dipped. Why should it matter that he was informally pledged to another? *Because he is here beside me now.* She bit the inside of her cheek hard. Then, she'd called him over with a brashness better fitting her sister, Chloe. And because she had to say something, she managed to squeeze out a steady, "Oh." Mimicking his earlier, effortless movements,

Philippa attempted another stone. This one skipped once and then disappeared under the water.

"Here," he encouraged. Rising, he took her by the hand and pulled her to a stand.

"What...?" Her question died on a broken whisper as he positioned her once more between his legs. Oh, God in heaven. The hard wall of his chest. The oaken strength of his thighs. Her pulse raced, pounding loudly in her ears.

"I fear I'm not much of an instructor if I provide you with but one lesson and leave you on your way to skip stones."

His teasing words startled a laugh from her. "It's not your fault. I'm a rubbish stu—" Then, he brought her closer still, killing all mirth. Her lashes fluttered wildly. "Student," she finished weakly.

"Remember," he breathed against her ear, stirring a loose curl. "Hold the stone between your thumb and forefinger with your thumb on top," he guided her arm back. "Draw your arm like..."

Philippa angled herself in his arms and cast her gaze up.

A charged heat blazed between them and he swiftly covered her mouth with his.

When she'd been confined to bed during her many pregnancies, she'd stared out the window at the changing landscapes. The dull monotony of her never-changing days had been those volatile summer storms that had shaken the foundation of her husband's sprawling manor house. As Miles pulled her into his arms, drew her close, and angled his mouth over hers again and again, as though he sought to brand the taste of her on his lips, this moment was remarkably like those powerful storms.

Her lashes fluttered wildly again and she snaked her arms about his neck, pressing herself close, wanting to lose herself in the feel of his embrace. Miles parted her lips and boldly tangled her tongue in an age-old dance. Parrying, she met that forbidden rhythm. Heat pooled in her belly and she tightened her hold on Miles, scrabbling her fingers down his back. Never in all her miserable years of marriage had she felt this passion coursing through her, scorching every corner of her being. And now that she knew, she wanted this rapturous bliss to go on forever. She pressed herself against him, reveling in the hard thrust of his arousal against her belly. "Miles," she moaned, crying out, when he pulled away. Wanting more of him, she gripped his neck, drawing him back, but with firm, steady movements, he set her away. The distant thundering of hooves cut across the thick haze of desire blanketing her senses.

And horror unfurled in waves, blotting out the warmth of his embrace. *Oh, God.* Of course, there were freedoms permitted her as a widow, but she did not wish to be one of those wicked, wanton widows, attracting lascivious attentions and gossip.

In one quick movement, Miles positioned himself between her and the rider. Tall, dark, and in possession of irreverent eyes that matched his hardened grin, the man flicked a dismissive gaze over the marquess. If it weren't for the cynical glint in his brown irises, he might be otherwise handsome. But his suggestive stare stripped away anything redeeming in the man. His sharp focus remained fixed on Philippa. "Guilford," the man called out as he slowed his black mount to a walk.

Unbidden, she stepped closer to Miles, finding a solace in his strong, reassuring presence.

"Montfort," the marquess said with a tightness that belied the affable, charming man he'd been in their previous exchanges.

The man tipped his hat. "A very good morning, I'd say, isn't it?" A sardonic grin pulled at his lips.

Tension poured off Miles' frame. "Indeed."

The other man made no move to leave. Instead, he urged his mount closer. "The perfect time to…seek out time alone in the park." He turned his attention to Philippa. "And it is Lady Winston, is it not?"

Miles' muscles tightened and the black fabric of his coat bunched under his bicep.

Not allowing the rake with his jaded eyes to cow her, Philippa stepped out from behind Miles and tipped her chin up. "My lord," she said with the icy regal tones that Lady Jersey would be hard-pressed to not admire.

He passed cold, appreciative eyes over her once more, before bowing his head. "I will allow you both your…pleasures." With another icy smile, Lord Montfort nudged his horse onward.

"Philippa," Miles said quietly, a thread of apology in that one-word utterance.

She shook her head. "Do not," she said softly. His was the first kiss she'd ever known that had reached inside her and set her afire. She'd not have that ruined with regret. No doubt, all of London would be abuzz with the shameful widow. Philippa mustered a smile. "I *am* a widow." Even having been married, Society would never separate her name from her familial connection. Nor would she wish them to. Not when those same individuals had seen her own husband as a man of worth and honor.

Miles scowled and opened his mouth but whatever words he intended were killed by the appearance of Philippa's maid over by the clearing.

"My maid is here," she said needlessly.

He hesitated; a muscle jumped at the corner of his eye, hinting at the barely suppressed volatility.

"Will I see you again?" she ventured with a still unfamiliar boldness that sent her toes curling. "That is…I come here in the morning and I was wondering if, by chance, you also happened to be…" *You are rambling. Stop rambling, Philippa.* "That is, if I do happen to see you, then…"

Miles reached a hand out and brushed his knuckles down her cheek. "Yes," he confirmed with that husky warm promise that sent delicious shivers through her. Then, he dropped his arm and with long, purposeful strides, returned to his mount.

A short while later, he rode off and left.

With the marquess now gone, the perils of being seen so, slammed into her and Philippa's shoulders drooped.

This was bad. This was very bad, indeed.

CHAPTER 10

SEATED AT HIS DESK, A brandy clasped between his hands, Miles stared down into the contents of his glass…as he'd been sitting for the better part of an hour.

He'd never been a rogue. Nor had he aspired to the reputation. And yet, he'd kissed Philippa in the middle of Hyde Park without fear or worry of passersby. In doing so, he'd subjected the lady to possible whispers and attentions. He gripped the glass hard as Lord Montfort's cynical eyes slid into his mind.

The man had observed him and Philippa and assumed what any lord or lady passing by would have—that they were lovers. The *ton* would assume their embrace was nothing more than an exchange between a widow and a bachelor, nearing his thirtieth year. As such, they would be free to carry on that relationship and though there would be whispers, there would also be a casual acceptance of an affair between them.

He took a swallow of his drink and leaned back in his chair. Yet, the truth of it was, he didn't merely want an empty entanglement with the lady. He liked her. He enjoyed being with her and her willingness to speak about topics that moved beyond the weather and the enjoyment of a ball, as so many other women of his acquaintance were inclined to do.

He'd known her but two days and, somehow, from their first meeting, she'd clung to his thoughts and refused to shake free.

And now, having been discovered by Montfort, he, as a gentleman wished to do right by her. Philippa, with her unjaded eyes and honest words, was undeserving of Society's condemnation. But in one rash moment, fueled by his hunger for her, he'd demonstrated to the Montforts of the world that the lady was amenable to a dishonorable suit.

Miles cursed and swiped a hand over his face. No, the rakes and scoundrels would not take the time to peel back the layers to see who Philippa truly was. They wouldn't see a mother who actually took time to be with her children, when most ladies foisted their babes off on nursemaids and saw them but a handful of times. Instead, Montfort and all those black scoundrels would be content with nothing more than the image he and she had presented that morn.

Footsteps sounded outside his office door and he straightened.

His mother pushed the door open and stepped inside. "Miles," she said without preamble and drew the door shut behind her.

He tamped down a curse. The last thing he cared for in this moment was a discussion or debate about Miss Sybil Cunning. She stalked over with the determined stride of a military general and sat in the leather chair at the foot of his desk. "You are drinking," she observed, needlessly.

He lifted his glass in salute.

"It is early," she snapped.

Miles rolled his shoulders. "Given my nearly thirty years, I expect I am well past lectures on expected behaviors." Nor had he given her reason to question his judgment or actions.

She tightened her mouth. "This is about that widow, isn't it?"

He stiffened, but said nothing. She was his mother, but he'd not answer to her or defend the company he kept. "I do not know what you are—"

"Sybil and her mother were here earlier. And where were you when they visited? Hmm?" Ire snapped in her eyes.

"I'm not discussing this with you." He couldn't. Not when he didn't know what to make of this hold Philippa held over him.

"Do you still intend to marry Sybil?" his mother asked bluntly.

Miles attempted to drag forward the promise he'd made. Except, he'd not made a promise to the lady. He'd given his mother until his thirtieth birthday to fulfill his responsibilities as marquess and marry the lady if they were still, as of then, unwed. He raked a hand through his hair. "It is…complicated now," he settled for.

Silence blanketed the room, punctuated by the ticking of the ormolu clock atop his mantel.

"Complicated," his mother said in succinct tones that stretched out every one of the four syllables.

After taking another sip of his brandy, Miles set it down and leaned forward. "Mother," he began, folding his hands on the desk before him. "I promised if I was not wed—"

"And you are not," she bit out.

"—by my thirtieth birthday I would marry," he continued over her interruption. "No, even though there has been no formal courtship made or offer of marriage, I cannot now in good conscience bind myself to Sybil." His mother had been so driven to cement the connection between their families and her devotion to her goddaughter. But surely she'd see her son's happiness came first. He didn't know, given what she'd shared in her past, whether Philippa ever wished to marry but he knew three meetings with the lady were not enough.

His mother pressed her palms to her cheek. "You surely are not speaking of courting Lady Winston." Shock laced that statement.

"She is the daughter of a marquess," he said ignoring her question. The young woman at the park had spoken with revelry for her newly attained freedom. Such a woman wouldn't be eager to bind herself to another husband. His stomach knotted. Oh, the irony. That he should desire more, and the lady spoke of her previous marriage with the same tones of one relishing the hereafter. "Furthermore," he went on, "the lady is a countess by her own right." Surely his mother, who could see nothing beyond titles, would, at the least, appreciate those pieces; the ones he cared the least for. He cared about her smile and the way she'd tossed that embroidery frame at him.

"She is an Edgerton," she snapped. "And she cannot bear children."

He snorted and in one swallow, drained his glass. "That is a stretch, even for you, Mother," he said, climbing to his feet. He crossed over to the sideboard. He poured himself another glass and returned to his seat. "The lady has two children, proof of that lie." Even had there been truth to her claims, Miles would never allow such a detail to keep him from wedding a woman. He took another sip.

"The lady has two *daughters* and no fewer than eight pregnancies."

He choked on his swallow. Eight pregnancies? Surely not. She could not be more than…five and twenty years. "Impossible," he gritted out, disgust at the careless way in which his mother spoke of Philippa's life.

"Hardly impossible," she continued relentlessly. "She lost her husband more babes than she birthed."

Her words slammed into him like a kick to the gut. He concentrated on his breathing to keep from thinking of artless Philippa, enduring agony after agony.

"Nor did she have the decency to give the late earl an heir before his death."

The glass cracked under the pressure of his hand and he set it down carefully. Had his mother always been so singularly merciless in matters of marriage? Miles shoved back his chair so quickly, the legs scraped along the hardwood floor. He stalked over to the door.

"Miles?" his mother called out. "Wherever are you going?" she called after him.

"Out," he bit out. And with all her ruthless pronouncement and unfavorable words, she could go to hell.

SINCE SHE'D RETURNED EARLIER FROM Hyde Park, Philippa had entered the townhouse more than half-expecting a barrage of questions from Chloe and furious admonishments over what had transpired between her and Miles. Seated in the parlor with Chloe and Jane reading from their copies of Mrs. Wollstonecraft's works, Philippa bounced Violet on her knee and it became apparent… her secret was her own. For now.

She should be properly horrified. After all, she *was* proper. Yet, she could not bring herself to muster even a modicum of shame. How could she, when having failed to know even a glimmer of passion in the whole of her life? She'd been awakened to the fiery hungering that proved she was not incapable of that grand emotion. A small, secretive smile pulled at her lips and she dropped a kiss atop her daughter's curls. Violet squirmed and she shifted

Violet's slight form in her arms.

Mindful of her sister and sister-in-law reading in the chairs opposite, she sang softly.

Sing a song of sixpence,
A pocket full of rye.
Four and twenty blackbirds,
Baked in a pie.
When the pie was opened,
The birds began to sing;
Wasn't that a dainty dish,
To set before the—?

"The Marquess of Guilford to see Lady Winston."

Her voice cracked mid-note as she jerked her stare to the butler who stood framed in the room's entrance. Silence resounded, as the three ladies looked with varying degrees of shock and surprise to the servant. Through the charged silence, Violet babbled and clapped her hands excitedly.

Joseph cleared his throat and shifted on his feet. "Should I inform His Lordship, Her Ladyship is not receiving—?"

"I'll see him," her frantic voice peeled around the room. Heat pricked her skin at the attention now trained on her. Shifting Violet's body in her arms, Philippa climbed to her feet. "You may show His Lordship in," she said with the remarkable composure she'd practiced through the years.

As soon as the butler ducked out of the room, the ladies present sprang to action. Chloe hurried to collect the leather tomes scattered about the table. Jane rushed over to gather Violet. While the ladies set the room to rights, Chloe trained a questioning stare on Philippa.

She warmed under that scrutiny. "It is hardly significant," she said quickly. "I am sure he is simply here…" Her mind raced. Why *was* he here?

Chloe winged an eyebrow up and stared back with a mature knowingness that defied her younger years.

"Come along," Jane urged, carrying Violet in her arms.

With a smile, Chloe hurried out of the room after her sister-in-law.

The knowing eyes of her family now gone, she pressed her palms to her cheeks. He was here. After their meeting in Hyde Park and their kiss, he should come here…now? To what end? Mayhap he intended to make her an indecent offer?

She slid her eyes closed as a wave of heat went through her at the memory of his kiss. Why should that possibility both thrill her and fill her with an inexplicable disappointment? She was not the manner of woman who'd ever wished to marry again. She'd traveled along that perilous path. A powerful marquess, Miles would certainly require the requisite heir and a spare…things she could never give him, or any man. Not when her life would surely be forfeit from the perils of childbirth. As it was, she'd spent the bulk of her adult life pregnant. While Society had few expectations for a woman beyond birthing babes and advancing familial connections, Philippa longed to live for *more*.

Footsteps sounded in the hall and she slowed her rapidly spinning thoughts. Why should her mind go to marriage? Why, after but a handful of chance meetings…and a kiss…and the lesson he'd given her on how to skip rocks…and…

"The Marquess of Guilford," Joseph announced.

Miles filled the doorway; his tall, muscle-hewn frame the manner of masculine perfection memorialized in stone. Her heart fluttered. "Miles," she greeted as Joseph took his leave.

He stepped deeper into the room, passing his gaze around the ivory parlor. "Philippa," he murmured and clasped his hands at his back.

She wet her lips as he wandered over to the window that overlooked the London streets. A volatile energy filled the room. *Why is he here?* Disquieted by the silence, Philippa cleared her throat. "Would you care for—?"

"I regret that we were discovered," he said, removing his gaze from the crystal windowpane. Regret that they'd been discovered; not that he'd kissed her. Such a slight, minor distinction and, yet, an important one.

Except… She bunched the fabric of her skirts in her hands. "This is why you've come?"

"In part," he said quietly.

Of course, as a gentleman he'd come to make his apologies. Annoyance unfurled within her. Resentment that he should express regrets for that moment and that a gentlemanly sense of honor had driven him here. "There is nothing to apologize for," she said, letting her hands fall to her side. "I…" Heat scorched her body. Who knew one's entire body was capable of blushing? And yet, for years of modesty, she owned that fiery exchange they'd shared earlier. "I wanted your kiss," she said with resolve and she had passionately returned it.

Desire glinted in his green eyes. Then faded. His thick, ginger lashes shielding his eyes, he took a step toward her. "If you were not a widow—"

"But I am." Bells chimed at the back of her mind. Surely he saw that very important distinction?

"There would be expectations."

They would be married. Or she would be ruined. "But there isn't," she reminded him as he continued forward, his long legged stride eating away the distance.

"I'll not have your name sullied."

Her heart dipped. This is why he should come. Not to make apologies, but to hint at doing right by her. Frustration and regret warred inside, muddling her thoughts. She didn't wish to ruin whatever bond they'd forged these past days with propriety and properness. He was the first man who'd ever truly spoken to her. Asked her questions. Listened to her answers and frustration. Now, he'd come and sully those moments with talk of regrets and decorum; those same empty, emotionless sentiments that had defined her life. A sound of frustration escaped her. "I am—"

"A widow," he said quietly. "I understand that. But *you*, matter. I'd not see you become prey to ill-intentioned rakes and scoundrels who desire nothing from you beyond the pleasure to be had in your arms." Her heart tripped. In the whole of her life, she'd served a single purpose to so many—to marry a respectable gentleman. No one had stopped to say that she actually mattered. Her happiness. Her happiness, beyond any safety and security she might know. Philippa's throat worked.

"Is that why you are here?" she asked tentatively. "To do right by me?" She held her breath.

He hesitated, caressing his gaze over her face. "And if I were to say yes?" There was a gruff quality to his question she could not identify.

She looked past his shoulder to the curtained window he'd abandoned moments ago. The day her husband had died, she'd resolved to never, ever enter into one of those cold, empty unions. Not when, ultimately, the need gentlemen had for an heir to carry on their names could mean her certain death. What she'd not ever considered, known possible even, was that she was capable of feeling this maelstrom of wonderful, stirring emotions; desire, joy, serenity.

Yet, how long could those sentiments survive when a man offered for a woman out of some misguided sense of honor? They couldn't. A coldness stole through her.

Miles brushed his knuckle down her cheek, bringing her eyes to meet his. She gave him a sad smile.

"I was married six years." He stilled his gentle caress; his hand frozen. "It was a good match by Society's standards." Her lips pulled in a sad smile. Title and rank, all that mattered to the *ton*. "We were a proper, respectable couple." Philippa stepped away, mourning the loss of his touch as his hand fell to his side. She turned her palms up. "But I was not happy." She bit her lower lip hard. "And I can never, won't ever, marry again. So while your offer to do right by me is wonderfully noble, I must decline."

"Why?" his gruff question rumbled from deep in his chest.

She opened her mouth.

"Why were you unhappy?" he clarified.

She drew in a shuddery breath and looked to the empty doorway. "I don't…" Lords and ladies did not speak on these intimate matters. It wasn't good manners to let people inside, to let one's most closely guarded secrets come to light. But mayhap if she told him, then he'd understand why he needn't stand before her even now speaking of propriety and every other useful Societal sentiment.

"I served one purpose for my husband, Miles," she said at last. After years of bitterness and heartache, she was able to give those words life without breaking inside. She wandered behind the upholstered sofa, putting much needed distance between them. "As a noblemen, you require heirs." His expression darkened and, unable to take the potent emotion threatening to burn her, she directed her attention to the top of the sofa. She skimmed her fingertips over the satin fabric. "That was my husband's sole use for me." Philippa ceased her distracted movement and curled her hands tight over the top of the sofa. "The day he died," she drew in a shuddery breath, "I was free." That shameful, sinful whisper floated between them. "And I certainly will never marry again out of some gentleman's misbegotten sense of honor and propriety. Not when I know what those unions inevitably become."

Miles strode around the sofa and stopped at her shoulder. "Not every marriage need be that way."

How very peculiar to witness a gentleman so very optimistic on the forever joining of two people. "Perhaps for some," she whispered, lifting her shoulders in a slight shrug. "Two of my siblings are happily married," she acknowledged. A chill stole through her and she folded her arms and rubbed. For though her brothers had found love, her mother had found hell...as had Philippa. "I learned not only as a wife, but also as a daughter, the danger in any man having dominion over me." She breathed slowly. "This is a hell I'd not ever dare suffer through again."

Something dark lit his eyes and he opened his mouth, when a loud squeal cut across whatever words he'd utter.

"Miles!" Faith charged through the doorway and flew across the room. The boisterous girl skidded to a halt before him.

There should be suitable horror at the outwardly display. And a year ago, even months ago, there would have been. The year since Calvin's passing, her daughter had unfurled like a tight summer bloom, full of life and color, and she reveled in that beauty of her spirit.

"Lady Faith," Miles greeted with a grand bow that raised a giggle.

"Did you bring my mama flowers?"

Heat slapped her cheeks. "Faith," she chided.

"*Did* you?"

Miles dropped to a knee. "I am afraid I failed to do so. It is a matter I must promise to rectify in the future."

Her daughter gave a pleased nod. "And remember, pick from the bottom of the stem, otherwise Mama cannot put them in a vase and they do need water."

"Of course." He grinned. "Though I expect I might benefit from an additional lesson."

Oh, God. How wholly gentle and patient and kind he was with her daughter, when Faith's own father hadn't even wished to be bothered with talk of the girl. A sliver of her heart slipped free and fell forever into his unknowing hands.

Faith prattled on. "It will have to be in the morning because I have my lessons with Miss Cynthia."

"Ah, but the best flowers are to be picked at night."

She giggled. "You are silly," she said with a roll of her eyes. "Everyone knows flowers sleep at night."

"Ah," he said on a mysterious whisper, holding a finger up. "But not all flowers." The husky quality of his words held Philippa enthralled and she was sucked into the words the way he surely intended. "There are moonflowers. Have you ever heard of them?"

Her mouth rounded, Faith shook her head.

"They are flowers," Miles went on in hushed tones that effectively held her always-chatting daughter in silence. "That only bloom at night. They close during the day."

She flared her eyes. "You *do* know about flowers." There was awe coating her high sing-song tone.

He winked. "My sister enjoys gardening and sharing her knowledge with me." Of course, Miles Brookfield, the Marquess of Guilford, would be one of those devoted brothers to attend his sisters' interests. Her own brothers hadn't wished to be bothered with her or Chloe and certainly not enough to listen if she spoke of flowers or anything else…

Faith captured Miles' face between her hands in a gesture so reserved for a loving daughter and devoted father that Philippa's heart wrenched. "Then mayhap we will have to gather flowers at night, Miles. I would like to see them."

His hushed response was lost to her. Occasionally, Faith would nod and smile. Philippa captured her lower lip between her teeth and bit hard enough that the metallic tinge of blood filled her mouth. In this moment, she could almost convince herself that she and Faith and Violet could have those elusive gifts she'd long believed only fortunate ladies were lucky enough to receive.

And standing there, watching him so wholly effortless with her daughter, the truth trickled in like a quick moving poison. This was why she could never, ever marry Miles even if he did ask. Which he hadn't. A man so at ease around children deserved offspring of his own.

Anguish weighted her chest and she drew in a ragged breath. And another. But it did not ease the vise about her lungs. Once upon a different time, when she'd been a young lady just out in London, optimistic with stars in her eyes, mayhap she could have met Miles and life would have belonged to them. They could have shaped a future together, different than the one she'd lived.

But she hadn't. Instead, she'd been introduced to Calvin.

Yet, from her miserable marriage and for all her childbirths, she'd been blessed with Faith and Violet. She would never trade any of the agony of loss for those gifts.

And it was because of that, Philippa could never give Miles more. Ever.

CHAPTER 11

M̧ILES SAT AT HIS PRIVATE table at the back corner of White's, the same bottle of brandy he'd requested two hours earlier remained beside the untouched snifter.

After he'd taken his leave of Philippa, her haunted eyes and insistent words echoed around his mind; consuming his thoughts. ...*I can never, ever marry again. Even if you wish to do right by me...* He stared blankly out, unseeing the gentlemen seated about him.

She'd endured a cold, emotionless marriage. Which was not vastly different than so many of the unions between lords and ladies.

He'd never given proper thought to the expectations his mother put to him years earlier regarding Sybil Cunning. If they married, they would have a polite, companionable union. But was that enough?

Just days prior, he would have answered with a definitive yes. Now, after seeing Philippa again for a fourth time, he'd been forced to reconsider the promise he'd made regarding Sybil. If it hadn't been for Philippa, he would have not considered all the perils that came in wedding where one's heart was not engaged. The haunted glimmer in Philippa's eyes, the pain he saw there, ushered in questions and doubts. Could there ever truly be happiness in that staid, proper affair?

Tamping down an agonized groan, Miles grabbed the bottle and poured himself several fingerfuls of liquor. He thought better of it and then filled his glass to the brim.

He took a long, slow swallow, welcoming the sting as it burned a trail down his throat. But it did little to ease the pain weighting his chest. Her words hadn't been restricted to the hell she'd lived as a wife, but she'd also spoken of suffering…at the hands of her father. And had her daughter not entered, he would have asked every last bloody question. Fury lanced through him; an unholy desire to drag her dead father and husband from the grave and kill them dead all over again. Was it a wonder the lady would be suspect of any gentleman's motives? Himself included?

"I believe this is the first time I can recall a scowl from the always affable Marquess of Guilford."

At that familiar, dry drawl, Miles shot his head up. He set his glass aside. "Bainbridge." Surprise crept into his tone. The other man, devoted to his two children and hopelessly in love with his wife, was rarely one for their clubs.

Bainbridge dragged out a chair and claimed the opposite seat with all the austere command of a man born and bred to be a duke. A servant rushed over with a glass, but the young duke waved the man off. All the while, he kept his attention trained on Miles. "I've read of your own impressive rescue of a lady in Hyde Park earlier this week," he drawled, folding his arms at his broad chest. He quirked a very ducal eyebrow.

Years earlier, Bainbridge had set the Town abuzz when he'd rescued his now wife from the frozen Thames. "Hardly the manner of heroics evinced by some," he said dryly. This was the reason for the other man's visit, then.

"But enough to merit gossip, of course," the duke spoke with his disdain for Polite Society underscoring his every word.

Miles gave a brusque nod. Gossip he'd only fueled that morning by taking Philippa in his arms.

"The papers purport an illicit relationship." His friend drummed his gloved fingertips on his sleeves.

A wry smile creased Miles' lips. "Apparently, in my advancing years, I've acquired the reputation of rogue." The young duke had never been one to dance around matters. His statements were more demands than anything else. Most of the *ton* feared the man. Miles, however, had known him since he'd been a sullen, lonely boy at Eton. Miles then stood beside that man who'd sobbed at the loss of his wife during childbirth. His dry mirth faded. How easily he'd encouraged the other man to move past his sorrow, but how very near to becoming his late wife Philippa had been.

"Well?" Bainbridge demanded gruffly.

He sighed, not pretending to misunderstand the question there. "The lady is a widow. I found her daughter wandering in Hyde Park and returned her." *And I've since seen her three more times, after, drawn like one of those hopeless sailors at sea.*

The other man continued beating his fingers in that annoying staccato rhythm. "A lady you've since seen again?"

He frowned. "Her daughter forgot her book in the park."

"Of course," the young duke drawled.

Shifting in his seat under the speculative glint in Bainbridge's eyes, Miles added, "Furthermore, it would have been ungentlemanly to not visit and see after the lady's well-being."

The ghost of a smile hovered on Bainbridge's lips. "Indeed, not," he stretched out those three syllables. Then, the duke had plucked a lady from the frozen Thames and never called again. It was the lady who'd continually sought him out.

Whereas Miles couldn't bring Lady Philippa 'round to any real interest. *That isn't altogether true. Her breathless moans and soft pleas bespoke a woman not wholly immune to me.* Miles rolled his snifter between his hands.

"She's not solely a young widow you happened to meet though, is she?" the duke said with an astuteness that could only come from years of friendship.

He shook his head once. "She does not wish to marry," he said quietly. Even with the bond between him and Bainbridge, he could not bring himself to share the whispered words about her childhood. "She nearly…" Miles looked the other man squarely in the eye. "lost her life in childbirth."

The duke's expression grew shuttered. But for the faint muscle that jumped at the corner of his mouth, he gave no indication of his thoughts. In all Miles' urgings that the other man re-enter the living, he'd not ever given consideration to the horror and hell of getting a child on another woman. How, after such a loss, could one ever be the same? Naively, with his own largely uncomplicated until now life, he'd never had the foresight to truly think of the implications in marrying, particularly where Bainbridge had been concerned.

At his silence, Miles continued on. "As such," he said with a wave of his hand, "she's no desire to marry."

"Does she have no desire to marry? Or to suffer the hell of childbirth?" his friend asked, not missing a proverbial beat.

Miles frowned, momentarily stunned by the questions tossed at him. In all Philippa had shared, with all her revelations, how had he failed to piece together those very questions Bainbridge put to him, even now? "I…didn't think," he said, at last, shamed by his own admission.

Bainbridge shrugged his broad shoulders. "Those are entirely two different matters."

Surely Philippa saw the value of her life far greater than any risk for a potential heir? *Then, why would she?* a voice whispered. She's known you but a handful of days and the husband who'd treated her as more broodmare than wife for more than six years.

His friend put another question to him. "Would you be content in never having children if you married her?"

Only, they would have children. They would have Faith and Violet. Violet, a babe he'd still not met beyond a chance meeting in the park; a child with cherubic cheeks whom he wished to know with the same tender regard he'd come to appreciate Faith. Yes, there would be children. There would just be no male issue of his own. "I am not worried over the Guilford line," he said, truthful. Where most gentlemen, like the bastard of a husband Philippa had spoken of, desired nothing more than their male offspring, he'd no sense of urgency or even a need to carry on the line. There was his brother and there would be other Brookfield issue. Then there remained the whole bringing the lady around to knowing she could trust in him. Why should she after just a few days of knowing one another? "She does not wish to marry again," he said curtly.

Bainbridge lifted another black eyebrow. "You coaxed me into the living. You helped me find a new life with a wonderful woman. I expect you can muster sufficient charm to woo the young widow."

Woo her? His frown deepened as he recalled every word he'd uttered to Philippa. He'd spoken of respectability and preserving her honor. Miles swallowed a groan. A woman whose previous marriage had proven so disastrous, so cold, and empty… Whyever would she have responded favorably to his own poorly launched suit? Miles dragged a hand through his hair. Never before had he wished for being one of those charming lords with all the right words. Until this great blunder.

Bainbridge shoved back his chair and Miles looked up as the other man stood. "You are leaving, so quickly?" He pushed the bottle toward his friend.

"I merely came to ascertain your circumstances." Despite himself, Miles' lips pulled at that blunt honesty. Bainbridge pierced him with his hard stare. "And to tell you not to be a bloody fool."

Miles chuckled and lifted his hand. "Send my best to the duchess."

The young duke inclined his head once more and, laconic as always, quickly took his leave, ignoring the terrified stares shot his way.

Bainbridge gone, Miles returned to thoughts of Philippa. Bainbridge's words rattled around his mind. Following his earlier meeting with his mother, he'd departed for Philippa's residence. He'd convinced himself that his intentions were borne of nothing more than Montfort's poorly timed appearance. Now, with his own thoughts and now Bainbridge's company, he was forced to face the truth he'd denied until now. He wanted her. Now, how to prove to the lady that she wanted him in return?

CHAPTER 12

SINCE YESTERDAY, PHILIPPA HAD BEEN lulled into a false sense of calm…that her actions wouldn't be discovered and bandied around Society. Now, today, standing at her vanity facing a new day, she accepted the inevitability of the whispers.

For the cold-eyed gentleman in the park was the manner of dastard who'd bandy about such a juicy morsel of gossip regarding the recently widowed Lady Winston. And then all of Polite Society would have their assumptions confirmed—Lady Philippa was a wicked widow. There would be veiled innuendos and unveiled ones. There would be improper offers and scandalous, stolen caresses.

For a sliver of a moment, she considered feigning a megrim. Or an injured ankle. Or a horrible cold. Anything. Because surely, when she made her way downstairs, she'd be met with an outraged mother and Gabriel brandishing a copy of *The Times* with all her sins from Hyde Park inked out for the whole of the world to see.

She stared into her vanity mirror searching for the same frightened eyes that had stared back at her every day of her five and twenty years. Mayhap she *was* a wanton. For even with the inevitable demise of her name and reputation or the stern lectures from her brother and mother, she could not bring herself to regret Miles' kiss. It had been the single most romantic, passionate moment of her five and twenty years that she'd not trade.

Her gaze went to the book resting on her vanity and she picked it up. With Jane's recent encouragements rattling around her mind, she flipped through the leather volume and stopped on a page that had been marked by her sister-in-law.

…Women do not want power over men. They want power over themselves…

A knock sounded and she spun about. The inevitable. "E-enter," she called out.

Jane stepped into the room and closed the door behind her.

Some of the tension went out of her. If anyone would be without recrimination, it would be her bold-spirited, unapologetic sister-in-law. "Hello, Philippa," she said softly, coming over. "Your mother is asking for you."

Her earlier courage faltered. She'd spent so much of her life trying to gain the approval of her mother, her father, her brothers, and then husband; a fear of their disappointment had become an unwelcome part of who she was. "Thank you," she forced herself to say.

…Your eyes speak a tale of a woman of strength… Even if you do not see it in yourself. Which you should… Miles' words echoed around her mind and she firmed her jaw. She was a woman of her own now. She'd returned to her family's home because they'd asked her here, but she needn't stay and be subjected to admonishments like she was a child who didn't know her own mind. Nor would she hide away in her chambers any longer. Bringing her shoulders back, Philippa started for the door.

Jane placed herself in Philippa's path, halting her forward stride.

Philippa looked questioningly at the shorter woman.

"When I met your brother, I despised him."

She opened and closed her mouth several times. "Beg pardon?"

"Loathed him from the moment I met him," Jane clarified.

Having been away in the country during one of her many confinements, she'd not known the details of how her brothers, Gabriel or Alex's, marriages had come to be. Given the love she'd seen between Gabriel and his wife, however, she'd never dare suspect that there had ever been animosity.

"You look surprised," Jane said with a wry smile.

"I am," she conceded. "You seem very much in love." She furrowed her brow. Surely she'd not been wrong in her supposition.

"Oh, you are not wrong," Jane said, correctly interpreting her unspoken wonderings. "You see, I judged all men by the manner of person my own father was." The Duke of Ravenscourt. As the duke's illegitimate daughter, life could not have been an easy one for Jane and still, she'd become this magnificently strong woman. Appreciation stirred anew. Jane waved the box in her hand about. "The point I am trying to make, Philippa, is that your husband was cruel, I suspect?"

She stiffened. "How…" Her mind spun. "Why…?" How had this woman seen when not even her own sister or her mother or brothers had?

"You carry your sadness in your whole person," Jane said softly. "Or you did. These past few days, I've seen joy in you that I've not seen in the six months in which you've lived here."

Miles. Unable to meet her sister-in-law's gaze, she glanced down at her feet. She'd hidden her every emotion for so very long, she didn't know how to share that intimate truth.

"I do not know the struggles that were yours, Philippa," Jane said, taking one of Philippa's hands in hers. She gave it a slight squeeze and then released it. "And I only know the demons your brother has shared of his own hell. But sometimes, there is light and there is goodness and there is love…and good men. If you are fortunate enough to find one."

Men who'd pick blooms with her daughter and whisper of moonflowers in her good ear. Men who'd attempt to do right by a widow when Society would never expect it of him. Philippa clasped her hands together and stared at the interlocked digits. "What if you can't give a gentleman what he requires…?" Her cheeks warmed. "For an heir."

Her sister-in-law laughed softly, forcing Philippa's gaze up. "Then I expect he is not one of those good ones and you are better off without." She opened the box in her hands and drew out a thick gold chain. A heart filigree pendant dangled from the end, twisting and twirling on the strand. "I want you to have this," she murmured.

Philippa stared at the necklace. "It is lovely."

"There is a story behind this piece," Jane explained. "It was once given to me by the Duchess of Crawford when I was just married to your brother…and then shared with others, after." She stared down with a faraway look in her eyes, studying the pendant with an almost reverent expression. "The legend is the wearer will earn the heart of a duke, but what other women have found is that with it comes love."

Unease knotted Philippa's belly as Jane held the necklace out. She held her hands up imploringly. "I…" Cannot. Would not. Do not wish to. She didn't desire a duke or a husband… Or she hadn't… Now, since Miles, it had all become so very muddled.

Jane stepped back and stared patiently. Her meaning clear: the decision ultimately rested in Philippa's hands. And when nothing had truly rested in her power, this offering meant so very much. Even if it was a silly talisman worn by hopeful debutantes searching for a duke. Wordlessly, Philippa turned around and lifted the curls draped over her shoulders.

"I had to do a bit of work to find its whereabouts," Jane murmured as she settled the chain about Philippa's neck. The faint click of the clasp resounded in the quiet room. "There," she confirmed.

A sharp charge of heat singed Philippa's neck and she touched her hands to her throat. "Thank you," she said softly.

"Do not thank me." She held out her elbow. "Shall we?"

Philippa cleared her throat. "I'll join you shortly. I would pay a visit to the nursery, first." The other woman looked as though she wished to say something more, but with a smile, turned and took her leave.

With Jane gone, Philippa made her way from her room, down the long corridor to the nursery, thinking on her sister-in-law's words…about love and marriage. Those dreams she'd long since given up on for herself. Some women, such as Jane, were blessed with joyous unions and then others…well, others were Philippa. Women who, if they were fortunate, had children who could fill all the voids inside an aching heart.

For the past six years, all her mornings and most of her days were spent with her children. They'd been the sole focus of her existence and, in them, she found a calming peace. She pressed the handle of the nursery and paused.

Squeals of laughter reached through the wood panel and she pushed the door open. Faith sat on the floor and Violet tottered back and forth, ambling into the older girl's arms.

The sight of her daughters' joyous smiles and flushed cheeks, stirred happiness in her heart. It had been just them for so very long. While he'd been alive, Calvin had demanded decorum from his wife and daughter, and frowned on public displays of affection and mirth. Now, there was a house full of family who celebrated in her presence.

Faith looked up. "Mama," she cried and raced over. She hurled herself into Philippa's arms with such force, she knocked her back.

Laughing, Philippa righted them and held her daughter close. "I am going to take breakfast," she said, tweaking her nose. "To see if Cook's sticky buns are still warm." She dropped to a knee and opened her arms as Violet rushed forward. She closed her eyes a moment welcoming the reassuring weight of her daughter's small form.

"Mama," Violet cooed.

Her daughter skipped over to the stack of blocks she'd abandoned. "I've eaten. Violet and I are to visit the gardens with nurse."

"You've eaten?" she parroted, surprise creeping into her tone.

Since she'd been old enough to walk and seek out Philippa, her daughter had always come first to her chambers and they'd always taken their morning meal together. A little pang struck her chest. "Yes," Faith said loudly. "There are sticky buns," she said, her attention reserved for the tower she now devoted her attentions to.

Violet squirmed in Philippa's embrace, pushing back until Philippa set her on her unsteady feet once more. With slow, ambling steps, the baby rejoined her sister.

And Philippa was—forgotten.

Calling out another goodbye, her daughters remained fixed on their playing. Philippa backed out of the room, closing the door behind her. It wasn't that she wasn't happy about their enjoyment…it was just that…they'd had a morning routine.

…You are not just your children… As she walked through the halls on her way to the breakfast rooms, Jane's words danced once more around her mind and she frowned. For the truth was, motherhood had been the sole purpose of her existence these years. Only someday, her daughters would be gone and who would she be? Unnerved by that question of her far-distant future, she reached the breakfast room and entered.

Her mother sat beside Chloe, with Gabriel and Jane at the opposite end of the long mahogany table. Holding her breath, Philippa stepped further inside and braced for the sharp cries and furious demands. Except…

"Good morning, Philippa," Gabriel greeted.

He sipped his coffee and Mother attended her breakfast plate and… There was no grand display of disappointment. Philippa took a tentative step toward the sideboard. Was it possible Lord Montfort, the witness to her embrace with Miles, had said nothing?

"Gabriel," she said quietly and proceeded to fill a plate. She then carried it to the seat alongside Jane. After all, if questions of scandal were raised, a place beside her undaunted sister-in-law was the very place she wished to be. She settled a napkin on her lap and reached for her fork. Her eyes went to the copy of *The Times* beside her brother's dish and she momentarily froze. Wetting her lips, she crept her fingers toward that sheet. Her hand touched the edge of the paper just as she registered the absolute silence.

"Are you taking my copy of *The Times*?"

She blinked, fingers frozen like a child who'd been caught with her hand in Cook's pastries. "Uh…" Yes, yes she was. Then, isn't that how Gabriel, Alex, and mother had always seen her? As a fragile miss in need of protection? "You aren't really reading it though, are you?" she asked needlessly.

Surprise flashed in Gabriel's eyes. Approval in Jane's. And confusion in Mother's. Taking advantage of their distraction, Philippa cleared her throat and swiped the paper. And proceeded to skim her gaze over the page intently searching for two damning names. She opened the copy and skimmed. Surely she could not be so very fortunate that the gentleman would prove honorable and not share what he'd observed?

"I have Lady Audley coming again for tea," Mother said.

Of course that was intended for her. She tightened her mouth and continued her search.

"And her son," Mother added.

At the strident note in her determined mama's tone, she smiled, welcoming the concealment of the paper. "Are they?" Philippa replied, not taking her attention from her search. She flipped to the last page of *The Times*. Nothing. There was no mention. A giddy sense of relief filled her and she set it down.

"As I was saying," her mother said with a deepening frown. "I have Lady Audley coming over." Again.

"That is lovely," she said, picking up her fork and knife and pro-ceeded to carve a piece of breakfast ham. "Have a most wonderful visit."

Gabriel's lips twitched. Hmm. He was capable of smiling; once more proving his wife's powerful influence.

"I was asking you to join Lady Audley and I," her mother said impatiently.

"Were you?" she asked pausing, her fork midway to her mouth. "Forgive me. I must have failed to hear the request."

Jane raised her napkin to her mouth and dabbed at her lips, but not before Philippa detected the smile there. Chloe, however, made little attempt to hide her wide grin.

Their mother stitched her eyebrows into a single line. "Philippa?" Confusion wreathed that single word utterance.

"I am afraid I cannot join you," she said, looking to her still-grin-ning sister. "Chloe and I are to go shopping shortly." It was, after all, time to abandon her widow's weeds.

Joseph appeared in the doorway, with a silver tray and calling card. Philippa's heart gave a funny leap. "The Marchioness of Guil-ford to see Lady Winston."

A pin fall could be heard in the silent room. She furrowed her brow. Miles' mother?

"The Marchioness of Guilford?" her mother said, cutting into the confused silence.

...*Though there is no formal arrangement, just an expectation among two mothers...*

Philippa cleared her throat. "If you'll show her to the Ivory Par-lor?"

The butler nodded and hurried from the room.

"What business does the marchioness have with you?" Her mother furrowed her brow.

Philippa managed a wan smile. "I expect it is merely a social call," she said evenly. Who would have believed Philippa Gage capable of such ease in lying? "If you'll excuse me?" she asked and climbed to her feet. With smooth, effortless steps, she started for the front of the room. "Oh, Mother?" she began, turning around.

The marchioness inclined her head.

"Just so you are aware. I have *no* intention of marrying Lady

Audley's son." She looked to Gabriel. "Or anyone else my family wishes to pair me off with." With that, she ignored her brother's frown and took her leave of the breakfast room. Chloe's muffled laughter trailed behind her, that brief moment of levity only momentarily distracting.

When she was away from their silent scrutiny, she increased her stride, a vicious twisting in her belly confirmed what her mind already knew—the Marchioness of Guilford's was no social call. Certainly not at this time of day. Had the woman discovered Miles' honorable almost-offer?

Philippa turned at the end of the corridor and slowed her pace. Running her palms over the front of her skirts, she came to a stop outside the parlor and plastered a smile on her face. "My lady," she said with false cheer as she entered. "How—?"

The marchioness climbed to her feet. "Lady Winston," she said quickly, wringing her hands. Worry wreathed her wrinkled cheeks.

Philippa motioned her to sit. "Please—"

"Lady Winston, I will not beat around the bush," the older woman said as she settled onto the edge of the ivory sofa. She continued to wring her hands. Philippa's stomach dipped. "I am here regarding my son," the marchioness said, at last confirming her suspicions.

Philippa slid into the seat across from Miles' mother and, with the hard glint in the woman's eyes, Philippa was once again the tongue-tied, speechless lady without any bold rejoinders. All the old frustrations with herself came rushing back.

The woman ceased her distracted movements and held Philippa's gaze. "I have read the scandal pages linking your names." Her breath froze in her chest. Oh, God, had she been discovered in that public embrace? She curled her toes in the soles of her slippers. "My son is an honorable gentleman." Philippa stiffened. "He pledged to wed my goddaughter, his distant cousin, if he was not wed by thirty."

"I do not see how this is any of my affair, my lady," she said in succinct tones, proud of that smooth deliverance.

The marchioness edged forward turning her hands up. "Don't you see, this is very much about you, Lady Winston? My son is a marquess."

Philippa set her teeth. "I know very well his title, my lady."

Miles' mother pounced. "Then you should also realize my son requires an heir and I wish to see him happy."

Were those two mutually exclusive? Or could Miles be a man who would equate that all-important heir with his ultimate happiness? Her stomach flipped over itself. At her silence, the marchioness seized full control of the discussion that was really no discussion at all.

"There have been…whispers of your circumstances," the marchioness went on when Philippa remained silent.

"My circumstances," she repeated dumbly.

The woman cleared her throat. "Your inability to produce heirs."

Bitterness lanced her heart, melded with a burning resentment that anyone should feel so bold as to ask questions where they had no right. "Ahh," Philippa managed. Is that what the *ton* should call the countless times she'd lain bleeding and weak, nearly dead for her efforts to bring forth that precious heir? She favored the woman with a stony silence.

"If the rumors are, in fact, just that…rumors," she searched her gaze over Philippa's face. "Then I would, at the very least, entertain the possibility of a match between you and my son."

Entertain a match? This stranger would enter Philippa's home and put bold demands and inquiries to her. Yet again, another person who the only worth they saw in Philippa was in her ability or inability to birth a boy babe.

All of Miles' beautiful lessons he'd unknowingly handed Philippa on her own strength and worth brought her shoulders back with pride. Mayhap it was years of abuse at her father's hands. Or the rigid expectations placed on her by her mother, husband, and brother, but Philippa's patience cracked. "How dare you?" she demanded.

The marchioness creased her brow. "I beg your pardon?"

"As you should," Philippa bit out, deliberately misinterpreting the other woman's words. "You come into my home and ask me to explain my connection to your son." Color flooded the marchioness' cheeks. "You expect me to speak about personal matters you have no right to ask on, with the only concern being your son's need for an heir." She surged to her feet with such alacrity her skirts snapped noisily at her feet. "I will tell you this, madam, I do not intend to marry your son." Nor had he asked. A slight exhalation of relief burst from the other woman's lips. "But even if I did, I would not answer to you about it. I owe no explanations, nor do I seek your approval. Now," she said, gesturing to the door, "if you'll excuse me? We are through here."

The older woman opened and closed her mouth like a trout yanked from the lake and tossed to shore. Then with stiff, regal elegance befitting a queen, she came to her feet. "Well, then," she said tightly. "With your deplorable manners you have proven you are very much an Edgerton." Yanking at her skirts, Miles' mother started for the door.

Philippa steeled her jaw. An Edgerton. The marchioness spoke it as though it was a sin upon her character, when in actuality, the Edgertons were something far more; something she'd failed to realize of herself—until this moment.

They were survivors.

And they would not be trampled by life…and this woman would most certainly not cow her. "Madam," she called out and the woman halted in her tracks. "My family demonstrates far greater dignity and grace than most." The marchioness brought her shoulders back. "And Society may whisper of us, but neither are we the manner of people who would dare enter someone else's home and call into question their character and worth." For as good, kind, and worthy as Miles had proven himself to be these past four days, his mother had demonstrated herself to be as cold as the rest of the *ton*. "Good day, madam," she bit out, not allowing the hated woman to raise all her oldest insecurities about bearing babes.

"How dare you?" the marchioness seethed, taking a step toward Philippa.

"No, how dare you?"

As one, they looked to the sharp exclamation that came from the front of the room. Philippa's mouth fell open. Fury radiating in her eyes, her mother rushed forward in a whish of skirts like a warrior storming a keep. "My daughter, the Countess of Winston, has asked you to leave and I insist that you do so this instant."

If the Marchioness of Guilford's cheeks turned any redder, she'd be set ablaze. "In all my years, I have never—"

"I will not ask you again." The Dowager Marchioness of Waverly's voice shook with emotion; more passion and life than she'd ever shown in the years she'd spent married to her miserable husband.

Through the years of her husband's abuse, never had her mother found the courage to intervene on behalf of her children—until now. So much love filled Philippa's throat, it choked off words.

"Well." With another flick of her skirts, Miles' mother stalked from the room.

The moment she left, the fight went out of Philippa and she buried her face in her hands. And in this instance, she couldn't sort out whom she hated more—herself for having a body that had so failed her, Miles' mother for being so very correct in him deserving a wife who could and would give him those boy babes he required, or Miles himself for showing her everything she'd never believed possible; dangling the sliver of a promise before her. All the while, knowing he could never be hers for every blasted reason his mother had spit out.

Her mother touched a delicate hand to her shoulder and she let her hands fall to her side. Tears glazed her mother's eyes. "I am so very proud of you. You have always been stronger than I ever could have hoped to be."

…your eyes speak a tale of a woman of strength… Even if you do not see it in yourself… With Miles' words whispering around her memory, Philippa offered a tremulous smile.

"I am so sorry I failed you," her mother whispered. "You deserved my protection from your father. Each of you did."

"You did not fail us. You did the best you were able. Just as I did with Calvin."

Shock registered in the older woman's eyes. Then, the dowager marchioness placed her fingers to tremulous lips. "Thank you."

And there was an absolution in that; freeing her mother of guilt and finding freedom in it herself.

"Oh, Philippa!" She jerked her gaze to the doorway where her sister and sister-in-law stood. Chloe's wide smile reached her eyes as she rushed forward. "You were brilliant." She took her hands in her own and gave a squeeze. "We were listening at keyholes," she explained. "And, Mother, you were utterly magnificent."

Their mother claimed Philippa's hands in hers and squeezed. "Your *sister* was magnificent." She looked over to Chloe. "As all of my children are."

All these years, Philippa had lamented that she was not more like her sister; strong, unwavering, fearless. Only to find out that Miles had, in fact, been correct.

She was far stronger than she'd ever credited.

Philippa smiled.

And before she left for the country and Miles was forever gone from her life, she would steal one more moment between them. That would be memory enough to live with her forever.

It would have to be.

CHAPTER 13

STANDING BEHIND THE SCAMOZZI COLUMN in Lord and Lady Essex's ballroom in the vibrant purple satin dress recently selected with Chloe, Philippa came to a new revelation. Apparently, the expectation was that young widows were only a *little* sad. The larger expectation from others was that she was in the market for a lover. *Then, when I'm caught embracing a gentleman in the middle of Hyde Park, how should anyone expect anything different?* Donning a gown with a deep décolletage did little to quell those assumptions, either. Her belly knotted. She'd not let them steal the simple joy in picking out the gown of her choosing. Societal expectations had already stolen enough of her happiness.

Just then, her gaze collided with a boldly staring Lord Montfort. A licentious smile turned his lips and she quickly stepped behind the pillar, heart racing. She peeked around the white column. Lord Improper-Eyes, as she'd dubbed him earlier that evening, skimmed the crowd and then found her once more. With a silent curse, she ducked behind the pillar again. Blasted gentleman.

Then, not all gentlemen are surely wicked. *There was one who helped my daughter and paid a call and asked her questions…questions that hadn't pertained to my interest in a lover.* A man who'd kissed her days earlier and whom she'd not seen since.

Her heart danced a funny little beat as a tall, commanding figure entered Lord Essex's ballroom. The hundreds of lit candles cast a soft glow upon his ginger tresses. Hugging herself close to the column, she secretly observed him as he strode with long, confident steps down the sweeping staircase. His path was intercepted by the Duke and Duchess of Bainbridge. Philippa watched on as the trio spoke with an easy familiarity. Occasionally, Miles tossed his head back on a laugh. He wore a smile. In every time she'd seen him, he did. Which was so at odds with everything she'd seen or known of her own stern-faced husband.

Her brother, Alex, a rogue, had long donned a false smile. Gabriel, hardly any at all, until his recent marriage. And yet, this man did. She'd not even known it possible.

He stiffened and then looked over the duke's shoulder. Their eyes met.

A thrill went coursing through her; an inexplicable pull that froze the breath in her lungs. He dipped his head in a silent greeting; that sincere, half-grin on his lips. And mayhap she was one of those scandalous widows after all, for she lifted her fingers in a slight salutation.

A despised figure stepped between them, immediately shattering that slight, maddening connection and she quickly sank back. She hardened her mouth, staring at Miles' mother. The same woman who'd entered her home yesterday morn and asked questions she had no right to. It was not, however, the nasty marchioness who earned her notice but rather the lovely blonde woman at her side. But for her spectacles, with her plump cheeks and golden curls, she may as well have been any other English lady in the room, and yet…there was an ease and comfort with which she spoke to Miles. Jealousy, sharp, gritty, and real, dug its sharp claws into her.

This was the woman. This was the lady his mother would see Miles wed. A woman, as she'd pointed out, who would give him children when Philippa would never traverse that dangerous path. Pain clogged her throat and she swallowed past the sizeable lump. It was why, even hating Miles' mother for the bold words she'd uttered yesterday, she saw the truth in those words, as well. She touched her fingers to the pendant hanging at her throat.

Silly talisman. Though beautiful in what it symbolized, it was foolish for her to have even donned the gift as anything other than a lovely ornamentation given her by Jane. Philippa would not know the love of a man. It was one of those foolish, empty dreams she'd tricked herself into believing might exist for her.

The gray-haired marchioness stepped aside, motioning to the dance floor, and Miles found Philippa briefly with his gaze. With the distance between them, she could not make out the emotion in his eyes. Then he returned his attention to the woman singlehandedly selected by his mother and escorted the lady onto the floor for the next set. As the orchestra's strands of the waltz soared about the room, couples twirled by in a violent explosion of vibrant gowns and tailed jackets. Young ladies with bright, innocent eyes and cheeks flushed with excitement. Yet, only one particular smiling couple earned her notice.

Miles easily guided the bespectacled woman through the motions of the waltz. Philippa tore her stare away from that perfectly paired couple and looked at the sea of smiling debutantes. *Was I ever that innocent?* Long ago, she'd been...

She closed her eyes a moment. As a girl of five who'd first suffered a birch rod being applied to her back by a father determined to beat obedience into his children, her innocence had been shattered. And yet...she opened her eyes, seeing those other ladies; hopeful and eager. And yet, for the horror of her childhood, hope had still dwelled inside. It was as Jane had only just opened her eyes to the fact that not all men were her father.

There were, in fact, gentlemen who were good and caring; capable of treating a woman and child with kindness and love when she and her own mother had known nothing but pain.

Philippa bit down hard on the inside of her lower lip. She'd been so determined to marry a man who was nothing like her father, she'd been deceived by a man's pretty words and the reputation he'd established amongst Polite Society. And through that folly, she'd invariably become her mother, albeit in a slightly different way.

Then she'd met Miles and everything she'd ever believed had been flipped on its ear.

"There you are."

A gasp exploded from her lips and she spun so quickly she lost her balance. Chloe shot her hands out and quickly steadied her. "Chloe," she chided, faintly breathless. "You startled me."

"Mother is looking for you."

She swallowed another very un-Philippa like curse. Of course she was.

Following her unspoken thoughts, her sister discreetly motioned across the room. "She is alongside Lady Audley."

Her stomach dipped. Of course, even with her bold rejection of those intentions yesterday at breakfast, her mother was relentless in her matchmaking pursuits. Why should she not bother with Chloe who'd, as of yet, been spared that miserable state? Not that she wished it upon Chloe. Anything but. She did, however, know Chloe would never be so weak as to make the same follies she herself had.

"Are you hiding from Mother? Or the crowd in general?"

Her sister's question startled her back to the moment. Philippa smiled. It was hard to not have a smile for Chloe who, with her frankness and strength, represented everything Philippa had never been but had always hoped to be. She dropped her voice to a conspiratorial whisper. "Perhaps, both?"

Her sister rounded her eyes and then a sharp bark of honest laughter spilled past her lips. "I've never known you to jest," she said as her mirth subsided.

Philippa grimaced. Yes, just as she'd never challenged her parents or husband, so too had she never done something as scandalous as make jests. Alas... The recent opinion of the *ton* was that she must be wanton. The whole widow business and all. Unbidden, she searched the floor and her gaze collided with Lord Improper-Eyes.

Chloe followed her stare and frowned. "Ah, so that is who you are avoiding. Lord Montfort," her sister supplied. "A notorious rake and highly improper." She spoke the way a seasoned match-maker who knew the most suitable matches a lady should hope to make. She softly cursed. "He is coming this way now." Philippa's stomach dipped. In all her greatest horror of reentering London Society, she'd not given thought that she would be sought after by men with dishonorable intentions. "Go," Chloe said from the corner of her mouth.

Philippa looked at her. Go?

Her sister waved a hand. "You are free to slink about your host's home, while we unmarried ladies face ruin for something as scandalous as escaping the ballroom." She looked out across the ballroom once more. "Or stay. Mother is on her way now with Lord Matthew, which I expect is far less safe than the Earl of Mont—"

Philippa spun on her heel and, keeping to the perimeter of the ballroom, marched along the crowded room. She took care to avoid the less than honorable eyes being cast her way. With every step, pressure built in her chest. Who would have expected that this misery would be far more oppressive than the dance to secure a husband all those years ago? She reached the back of the ballroom and without hesitating, rushed from the room and continued walking until the cacophony of the festivities was a muted in her ears.

She'd never done something so outrageous as slipping about her host's home. As a debutante, she'd stood demurely and obediently at her mother's side. As a wife, she'd spent more time in the country, confined to a bed, attempting to give her late husband his precious heir.

With each step, a lightness filled her. A giddy sensation that threatened to carry her away from the misery of all these stilted affairs and her family's oppressive attentions. Footsteps sounded from somewhere in the townhouse and her heart skipped a beat.

Philippa made a grab for the nearest door handle, pressed it open, and slid inside. Heart hammering, she drew the door closed and leaned against the solid wood panel. She blinked, giving her eyes a moment to adjust to the darkened space; the broad, mahogany desk, the heavy, well-stocked sideboard. It may as well have been any other nobleman's study.

Some of the tension left her at the silence ringing in her ears and she strolled over to the crystal decanters lining the piece of furniture. Absently, Philippa picked up a bottle.

…He does not drink and he does not wager… He'll make you a proper husband…

Her fingers shook with the remembrance of Gabriel's assurances all those years ago and she quickly set the crystal down. How very erroneous he'd been. How utterly and absolutely flawed. To believe that Lord Winston, with all the right words and the proper image crafted by Society, was somehow honorable for that image. Hadn't the Edgertons learned long ago that any nobleman could expertly present a façade to the world? Her lips twisted with bitter cynicism and she thrust aside the unwelcome memories of her childhood.

There was no place for them. Just as there was no place for

regrets. And with the dream she'd long carried, of having the love and kindness of a devoted husband, long since dead…the love of her children would forever be enough.

For her.

Philippa tightened her mouth. To Mother and those lecherous gentlemen eying her, they'd seen a woman alone and deduced that she desired something more.

And since she was, for the first time in her life, being honest with herself, she admitted they were right.

She wanted one night in Miles' arms.

CHAPTER 14

℘WHERE IN BLAZES HAD SHE gone?

From over the top of his dance partner, Sybil Cunning's head, he did a search for Philippa. Alas, she'd abandoned her position at the broad pillar. Had she been hiding there? Or was she even now waltzing in some other gentleman's arms? He hardened his mouth and continued looking.

"…Did you see my mother took flight in the middle of the ballroom…?"

"Hmm?" Had some prospective suitor caught her notice or some rake with dishonorable intentions? Montfort mayhap?

"Oh, yes. And she intends to overthrow the king and name herself monarch."

Miles blinked and yanked his attention down to Sybil. Plump, with full cheeks and a rounded form, she wore one of her patent smiles that always reached her eyes. In this moment, through the crystal lenses of her spectacles, mischief danced in their brown depths. He blinked several times. "Beg pardon, Sybil."

The young woman, in her twenty-eighth year, snorted. "In the whole of my life, I've never known you to woolgather."

No, he'd always been rather practical. There had been no reason to woolgather. And no woman to woolgather over. Until now.

"You're doing it again," Sybil pointed out with a widening smile.

He gave his head a hard shake. What spell had Philippa woven in these past days? Miles sighed. "Forgive me," he apologized. "My mind was otherwise occupied." As it had been since she'd stumbled down that walking path and into his life.

"Is it Lady Winston, then?" Curiosity underscored Sybil's inquiry. Miles stiffened.

"The woman who's at last captured your heart."

His mind came to a screeching halt. "I..." Had no suitable reply. For though there had been no spoken, or even unspoken, pledge between them, there had been a silent understanding among two children of friendly families.

With another inelegant snort, Sybil slapped his arm. "Oh, come, Miles. I've known you since we were babes. Never before has your name filled the scandal sheets...until this week."

As he guided Sybil through the steps of the waltz, he carefully picked his way around, searching for a suitable reply. The actuality was, if he hadn't met Philippa that day in the park, he would have married Sybil in two weeks' time and they would have been happy. Politely so. There was not, nor would there ever have been passion, or this gripping mastery of his mind and heart that Philippa had managed.

He sighed. Sybil deserved more of him than a public confession in the midst of Lord Essex's ballroom and, yet, she deserved something of him. An explanation. "It is Lady Winston," he conceded.

"I knew it," she said with another wide smile. She let out a long sigh. "Thank goodness."

He cocked his head. "Thank goodness?"

"Surely you do not think me oblivious to our mothers' scheming these years, hmm?"

A flush climbed up his neck.

She flashed him a wounded look. "I am disappointed, Miles. Knowing me as you once did and, yet, you think me so empty-headed that I'd be so oblivious to their frequent talks of us marrying."

Miles guided her in another smooth circle. "They wished to see us happy," he said. That, however, did not excuse their mothers' interfering in her life...or his. In making that pledge to his mother, he was just as guilty.

"They wished to see us married," she said bluntly. "But no one ever thought to my happiness." She gave him a long look. "Not even you in offering to marry me...is it before your thirtieth birthday, hmm?"

He managed a sheepish grin. "Yes, well, you are correct. Virtue can only flourish amongst equals."

Sybil flared her eyes. "Are you quoting Mrs. Wollstonecraft, now?"

"I am, thanks to a wondrous, much needed influence in my life." Philippa had changed him in ways he'd not known he needed changing.

"Thank you," Sybil said with a soft smile. "I am grateful for not only your offer, but also your wisdom in finally seeing what I desire matters just as much. I never wished to marry a man who did so for a sense of familial obligation. I'd rather marry a man who searched around the ballroom for a sight of me." She dropped her voice to a conspiratorial whisper. "She snuck out the back entrance."

He swiveled his head around and promptly missed a beat trampling his partner's toes. "Forgive me," he said quickly, restoring his attention. Where had she gone off to and for what end?

As the orchestra ceased playing, Miles brought them to a halt. He passed his gaze over Sybil's face. "Thank you," he said quietly. "You deserved a far better husband than me, anyway."

She blushed. "Oh, hush. You were never one of those flirty sorts," she said as he escorted her from the floor. "Just as you weren't one of those scandalous sorts. For if you were, I'd expect you'd go after your lady."

Miles winked, earning a laugh. As her amusement faded, he gave her another look. "Thank—"

"If you thank me again, I'm going to clout you over the head. Now go," she said. "Go," she repeated with a gentle insistence.

With a bow, he turned on his heel and made his way through the guests. Slipping out the back entrance of the ballroom, he made his way down the darkened corridors. His footsteps silenced by the thick carpet, he did a quick search of the rooms along the hall. He pushed open another door and stopped. Moonlight filtered through the crack in the curtains and bathed the room in a soft glow.

From where she stood at the sideboard, Philippa stared back. He ran his gaze over her slender frame, draped in shimmering purple satin. "Miles." Surprise threaded her greeting.

He stepped into the room and pulled the door closed behind him. "We meet again, my lady."

The last place Miles, the Marquess of Guilford, should be was in Lord Essex's private study with the young widow and her midnight tresses. If they were discovered, there would be no expectations of marriage the way there would had she been an unmarried miss. There would, however, be assumptions—about her as a young widow and him as a still unmarried gentleman.

Only, whenever Philippa was near, the world with all its staid expectations ceased to matter. He could only see her—just as he had from the moment she'd came racing down the riding trail in Hyde Park. Miles pushed away from the door and started over to her.

SHE SHOULD NOT BE HERE. Given her meeting yesterday morning with Miles' mother and her observation of him with the woman who would, no doubt, one day be his wife, they had no place being alone as they were now.

For even as she wished to be with him, cared for him, desired him, she could not be one of those wanton women who would ever come between him and his eventual wife. Philippa studied the tips of her slippers. "You should not be here, Miles."

"Why?" His husky baritone wrapped around that question and sent heat spiraling inside.

"Your Miss Cunning." A woman, perfectly plump and golden blonde and all things an English lady should be. No doubt, she'd give Miles perfect, flawless babes and they'd be a laughing, joyous family, and… A spasm contorted her chest.

She stiffened, as Miles dusted his knuckles along her cheek. "Is that the manner of man you take me for?" There was a hard, wounded edge to his question that brought her gaze snapping up to meet his. "Do you take me for a gentleman who'd seek out one woman while intending to betroth myself to another?"

"No," she said on a rush. "Of course not." The oddity of it all was that, even knowing him just these few days, she could say beyond a doubt that Miles Brookfield was a man of honor. The woman fortunate to have him as her husband would have a devoted, loving man at her side. And God, how she despised that eventual lady.

He continued stroking her cheek. "And yet, you believe I would be here if my intentions were to marry another?"

…*My intentions to marry another*… Words that suggested his intentions to wed her. Philippa's throat worked spasmodically. She would never have anything more to do with him. And that truth was not borne of his mother's meddling, but rather a truth of who *she* was. In a Society where dutiful wives gave their husbands many babes, boys with which to carry on that distinguished title, she could never give him those things. Nor would she ask him to abandon those gifts that all men wanted.

But she would know his kiss once more.

Miles peered at her through thick, hooded lashes. "What are you thinking?"

She trailed the tip of her tongue along her lower lip and his gaze went to that slight movement. Desire flared in the endless green depths of his eyes and a heady sense of feminine power gripped her. "I want you to kiss me," she whispered.

His body jerked as though he'd been struck and then with a long, agonized groan, he took her in his arms. With his mouth, he devoured hers in a meeting that was fierce and hard. He slanted his lips over hers again and again, a primitive male wishing to forever mark his mate, and a low moan slipped from her throat as her lips parted to allow the sound to escape. He took advantage of that slight movement and thrust his tongue into her mouth, where she tangled her tongue with his; sparring in a forbidden dance. With raspy breath filling the quiet of the room, Miles cupped his hands about her buttocks and dragged her close. The thick length of his desire prodded her belly, liquefying her with a white, hot heat.

In this moment, Philippa forgot all the reasons there could never be anything more with him and, instead, took this gift of passion he offered. He drew his mouth back and she cried out softly at the loss of him, but he merely ran his lips down her neck, sucking and nipping, and finding her pulse pounding away at a maddening rhythm. With a ragged moan, she clasped her fingers reflexively in the silken tresses of his unfashionably long, ginger hair.

"I want you, Philippa," he breathed raggedly against her skin as he dragged his mouth on a scorching path from her neck to her décolletage. Her knees buckled and he guided her against the sideboard.

"Miles," she whimpered, as he freed her breasts from her gown. The cool night air slapped her heated skin in a delicious mix of hot and cold. He cupped the white mounds in his hands, pushing them together, and weighing them. Moisture pooled at her center and she reflexively arched her hips, needing this gift he held out—pleasure, desire, hunger—all those wickedly wonderful sensations she'd believed herself incapable of. Then he raised a breast to his mouth. His hot breath fanned the skin and the tip puckered under his mastery. She slid her eyes closed as he drew the bud between his lips and suckled. That skillfully seductive act pulled her into a sea of sensation where she was reduced to a bundle of thrumming nerves. Never, ever in any of the times Calvin had visited her bed and fumbled through their couplings had she burned with the need for his touch.

She bit her lip to keep from crying out and tangled her fingers in his hair, anchoring him close, never wanting him to cease his delicious torment. "Please," she managed to pant out.

Miles showed no mercy. He dropped to his knees and slowly drew her skirts up, so that the air caressed her skin. "Let me love you," he whispered, trailing kisses along her calf, up the sensitive flesh of her inner thigh. His hot breath stirred her core and she whimpered, burning in ways she'd never felt. Knowing only Miles could teach her.

"Wh-what…?" she whispered as he put his mouth to her mound. His breath stirred the curls shielding her femininity and her entire body jerked. "Miles," she rasped.

He parted the curls and, with his lips, found her swollen nubbin. A low, tortured moan bubbled past her lips. She arched her hips toward him, aching for more of his wickedly wonderful ministrations. In the whole of her marriage, lovemaking had been mostly painful, always awkward, quick couplings she'd silently suffered through. With Miles, he'd awakened her to the truth that she was very much a woman; a woman capable of passion. And she wished to know all of his touch. Philippa let her legs fall open and she tangled her hands in his luxuriant hair as he thrust his tongue inside her.

He swirled his expert tongue around, playing with the pleasure nub. Then the way he'd done with her nipples moments ago, he sucked that flesh between his teeth. Her breath coming hard and fast, Philippa thrust herself against him. Tension spiraled inside her and she gritted her teeth, her body climbing toward an unknown precipice. Then, he reached between them and his fingers found her sodden center. She flared her eyes and on a sharp cry, exploded in a wave of color and feeling. Waves of ecstasy went rippling through her with such force and she wept from the force of her climax, arching and twisting, wanting the moment to go on into forever. Miles continued suckling her nub, until he'd wrung every last bit of utter bliss from her. She slumped on the sideboard, faintly panting.

Philippa slid her eyes closed, breathless from her exertions. As a wife, she'd been schooled by her miserable husband to believe their joining's served only one purpose—to produce his precious heir. There had never been satisfaction. As such, given the lessons handed down by her mother before she'd married on her "dutiful obligations" in the marriage bed and the shamefulness of that act between husband and wife, she should be scandalized. She should be ashamed and mortified and all those proper responses ingrained into her from early on.

Her breath settled into a smooth, even rhythm. And yet, in this, there was no shame. There was just a glorious sense of being alive and knowing the powerful wonder that her body was capable of. Pleasure she'd long believed herself incapable of knowing through a deficit in who she was as a woman. Miles placed a final kiss along the sensitive flesh of her inner thigh and drew back, adjusting her skirts and undergarments.

A tear slid down her cheek. "Thank you," she whispered. "I never knew... I never..." She sucked in another breath. "Thank you."

Miles caressed her cheek. "May I call on you tomorrow?" he asked, his meaning clear.

And just like that, reality intruded. The realness that was her life. She mustered a smile. "O-Of course." He wished to court her. And were she any other woman, a wholly unbroken woman, she'd have reveled in his attentions. But she was not. And, as his mother had coldly reminded her, never would be. With frenzied movements, Philippa set to work righting her gown. She then gathered the strands that had sprung free of her once neat chignon and attempted to stuff them into a semblance of order. "I have to return."

"I know," he whispered, touching his lips to her earlobe.

She moaned and leaned back into his caress. He angled her around and found her mouth with his. Their tongues met in the same fiery explosion they'd shared since their first embrace at the lake. It was Miles who found the fortitude to draw back.

Wordlessly, he turned her about once more, removed the butter-fly combs from her hair, and reworked the tresses. Everything he did was done with such infinite gentleness and tenderness that the remaining parts of her heart that hadn't already been claimed fell into his hands. "Until tomorrow," he promised.

With a shaky nod, Philippa rushed to the front of the room and left. Her heart thundered hard; the rapid beat filling her ears and as she fled, a panicky desperation filled her. She'd no doubt he would offer her his name and as she wanted him—all of him—she'd not force him to abandon what he required as a marquess.

She bit her lip hard and rushed around the corridor nearly to the entrance of the ballroom and collided with a hard, thick wall. Philippa grunted and reeled back, but a pair of large, strong hands shot out and righted her.

"Lady Philippa, how unexpected but utterly delightful meeting you here on the way to *your* assignation." By the slight emphasis, they were two ships sailing in the night.

Lord Montfort smiled. And this was not the easy, affable, sincere grin worn by Miles but rather a cold, empty expression of mirth. Her own existence had proven life indelibly shaped a person; marked you with pain. What was to account for this man's steely edge? Seeing it, recognizing it, however, made him more man than the beast she'd taken him for at Hyde Park. "My lord," she said quietly, glancing about. If she were discovered, there would be even more questions she didn't wish to answer. "If you'll excuse me?" She made to step around him when he called out, staying her.

"May I offer you a word of advice?"

What advice could a man with his hard eyes have for her? She eyed him warily.

"If you're prepared to sneak away for your pleasures, then do not make apologies for it. Take your pleasures where you would and be damned with anyone for their opinions."

Surprise filled her. From her first sighting of him in the park, she'd believed him capable of nothing but malice.

His wicked grin deepened. "If you are, however… amiable?" he whispered lowering his head closer.

Philippa leaned back and offered a wry smile. "I assure you, I am n—"

Footsteps sounded down the hall and they looked as one. "You bastard," Miles hissed, rushing forward. Philippa gasped as, in one quick movement, he hefted the earl away and leveled him with a single blow.

"Miles, no," she cried, reaching for his arm. For the earl's wicked offer, nothing untoward otherwise had happened.

With a grunt, the other man went down hard on his knees. "By God, Guilford, I didn't—" Coming over the earl's form, Miles punched him again.

"Oh, my goodness!"

That shocked exclamation filled the corridor and froze Miles mid-blow.

And then, with a sinking wave of horror, Philippa turned to the small audience that had gathered—Lady Jersey, Philippa's mother, Gabriel and his wife. Her brother narrowed a lethal stare on the two battling men.

She clenched her toes so hard, her arches ached.

"Lord Guilford," Gabriel drawled, his tone dripping ice.

His chest heaving from his exertions, Miles stood, mouth agape, staring at their audience.

Taking advantage of that distraction, the Earl of Montfort punched him in the face and Philippa cried out. "Only fair to return the favor," he said with the same humor of one discussing a Drury Lane comedy.

Several additional guests converged on the hallway and Philippa covered her face with her hands.

This was bad, indeed.

CHAPTER 15

IT HAD HAPPENED.

For the first time in his nearly thirty years, Miles had found himself on the front page of the scandal sheets. All of them, to be precise. The stack at the corner of his desk glared mockingly back. With a growl, he shifted his attention from the papers in front of him to those useless scraps. He swiped the top copy and skimmed.

The Wanton Widow of Winston finds herself fought over by the Marquess of G and the Earl of M...

The muscles of his stomach clenched into tight, painful knots and his fingers curled about the pages of the hated sheet. They would print her name for all to see, while providing him and that bastard Montfort at least the slight anonymity of a given initial. He crumpled the page into a ball and hurled it into the rubbish bin beside his desk. By God, he'd done this. With his carelessness yesterday and in Hyde Park, he'd subjected her to the whispers and stares and the advances of cads like Montfort.

Miles picked up his pen and tapped it distractedly on his papers. If she would trust in him, he would marry her, not just to do right by her...which he did want that, too, but because he loved her. He loved her spirit and strength. He loved her devotion to her daughters. And he wanted to be a family with her and Faith and Violet. A pressure weighted his chest. Yet, with the life she'd lived, the misery of her own marriage, and the details she'd only alluded to of her childhood, she had no grounds to want to marry him.

Never more had he wished to be one of those charming lords with all the right words.

The door flew open and he looked up. His mother stormed into his office and slammed the door behind him. "I've allowed you to shut yourself away in your office. Did you think I'd not expect you to speak on it?"

He swallowed a curse. "Mother," he drawled and tossed down his pen. No, he rather thought a woman who so wholly survived and thrived on gossip would not allow him to escape talk. "Actually I did," he said, rolling his shoulders. The last thing he cared to discuss was the scandal of being discovered alone with Philippa and bloodying Montfort for daring to put his hands on her. Another primal surge of bloodlust went through him at the memory of that bastard's mouth on hers.

"Are you listening to me, Miles?" she snapped.

"No, I am not," he said, eliciting another gasp. For the whole of his life, he'd been a dutiful son; seeing to the obligations and responsibilities that went with the Guilford title. He'd done so unflinchingly since his father had died ten years earlier. Where other lords had reveled in the freedom that came with being a bachelor in possession of great wealth, he'd dedicated himself to growing that wealth and never becoming one of those indolent lords. He'd not make apologies for any of his actions. And most especially, not for the feelings he had for Philippa.

"Do you know the scandal you've caused?" she implored. "What you've done to Sybil?"

"I have already spoken with Sybil. She understands my heart is otherwise engaged."

Silence fell over the room. A very short-lived silence. "What?" she barked, a seal-like quality to that one word.

He tamped down a sigh, taking some mercy on his mother. There had been the expectation and lifelong hope on her part that he would marry her goddaughter and cement their families. In time, she'd come to appreciate the manner of honorable, strong, woman Philippa was. "I am in love, Mother," he said quietly as silence resounded in the room. His body went still. *I love her.* He loved Philippa with everything he was. He loved her as a woman of strength. He loved her for being a devoted mother. And he'd spend every day filling her days with joy if she'd but have him.

His mother opened and closed her mouth. "But…but…"

Miles flexed his jaw, tired of her disparagement of Philippa. "I intend to marry her." Regardless of the expectations his mother had of or for Miles.

"You needn't marry her." His mother threw her hands up. "She is a widow."

A black curtain of rage descended over his vision, momentarily blinding him, and he quelled her with a glare. "Have a care. That woman will be your daughter-in-law." *If she'll have me.*

The marchioness sputtered. "Sh-she said she would not marry you. A liar and a wanton." She muttered that last part under her breath.

He froze. "What?"

"I said a liar and a…" At his black glare, her words trailed off. Color rushed his mother's cheeks and she slapped one palm against the other. "I paid Lady Philippa a visit a few days ago in order to ascertain the state of your affairs."

He choked. "You paid her a visit?" Fury and outrage gripped him. He thought of Philippa receiving his mother as a visitor and dealing with the woman's vitriol. "What did you say to her?" he demanded. "What did you say?" he boomed, when she remained unyielding.

She jumped. "I explained you required an heir. I sought to determine if she could give you that heir."

A growl worked up his chest and he let a vile curse fly, ignoring the way his mother gasped. He swiped his hand over his face. Philippa had endured a hellish marriage where her husband had seen her as nothing more than a broodmare for his babes. With her insensitive and bold questioning, his mother had demonstrated the same singular focus all Society held dear. Of all the unkindness Philippa had received, he'd now add his mother to one of those who'd done wrong by her. Regret pitted his belly. "Get out," he seethed.

His mother rocked back on her heels. "Miles?" she squeaked.

He shoved to his feet and layering his palms upon his desk, he leaned forward. "I am marrying her," he said again through hard lips. "And I will not allow you to disparage her. Are we clear, madam?"

She blinked.

"Are. We. Clear?" he bit out in succinct tones.

His mother gave a juddering nod.

And without another word or glance for his mother, he stalked from the room. He had a widow to woo.

CHAPTER 16

⁋IN THE LIGHT OF A new day, with her scandal gracing the front pages of every scandal sheet, Philippa came to a very powerful realization about her family—they were more forgiving of ill-behavior than she'd ever credited.

Following her hasty departure of Lord Essex's ballroom, she'd braced for a tide of stern admonishment and a flurry of tears from her mother. Alas, they'd ridden the whole of the carriage ride in silence with not a single word uttered. And when they'd arrived home and she'd been asked to meet them in Gabriel's office, she'd held her breath, waiting for the explosion.

That hadn't come. Instead, Gabriel had quietly informed her that the family would be retiring to the country and then the unthinkable had happened. He'd asked if she and her daughters would join them. Asked, when she'd only ever truly been ordered about. There should be a thrill of victory in that. There should be a sense of triumph that even with the scandal she'd brought down on the family last evening, they'd not admonished and lectured the way they had done for the whole of her life.

So where was the sense of victory? Instead, all she knew was this great, gaping hole in her heart. Her throat worked painfully and she pressed her eyes closed hard. For one week of her life, she had been so very happy and felt alive in ways she'd never, ever felt.

Because of him. Miles. She sucked in a pained breath and her chest throbbed with a dull ache. Philippa leaned her forehead against the smooth windowpane. In the streets below, servants carried the trunks to the three waiting carriages as the final preparations took place for their departure.

"My lady?" Releasing the curtain, Philippa spun around and faced the servant at the doorway. "His Lordship said it is time."

It is time.

Philippa struggled to drag forth a suitable thanks, but her throat constricted. Instead, touching her fingers to the silly pendant that hung about her throat, she managed a slight nod. The retreating footsteps and the faint click of the door as it closed filled the quiet. Philippa returned her attention to the activity below. Her maid finished filing away the last of her garments and then closed the trunk with a final, decisive click.

That click resonated with a finality that stabbed at her. It represented the end of the most gloriously romantic week she'd known in the whole of her existence. For when she boarded that carriage and departed for the country, a now scandalous widow, Miles' life would carry on as it had before her.

He would marry. Mayhap not his Sybil Cunning, but there would be another, a woman who, no doubt, deserved him more than Philippa ever could. Oh, God. Agony ripped through her and she hugged her arms close to her waist. And every day of her life she would hate the woman who called him husband; would hate her with a vicious envy that she should know the love of such a man.

She ignored the faint sound of the door opening and focused on breathing. Anything except this pain knifing slowly away at her insides. "Please inform my brother I will be down shortly," she said through clenched teeth.

"Oh, surprisingly, Gabriel is being exceedingly patient."

At Chloe's dry words, Philippa wheeled around. "Chloe," she said.

Her sister stepped aside for Philippa's maid. After the young woman had gone, Chloe pushed the door closed and came over. She stared at Philippa a long moment. "You were not happy. I thought you must have loved your husband…but you did not."

Philippa bit her inner lip hard and let her silence serve as her answer. Eyes usually filled with mischief and spirit, were now filled with agony. "Was he cruel to you?" she asked, her voice breaking.

"Was he like F-Father?"

That crack in a woman of such remarkable composure ripped at Philippa. "No," she said shaking her head and she, who'd long been the protected, became protector. "It was not a miserable marriage," she lied. She gave a small, sad smile. "But neither was it a happy one."

Chloe sucked in an audible breath. "I do not know what woman would willingly subject herself to such a state. If one's heart is not breaking from the cruelty of marriage, then it risks being broken at the loss of that person."

How very jaded her sister was. What a dark, sad view of love. *Then, wasn't I the very same before Miles?* "Not all men are Father," she said quietly, not letting her sister's gaze go. "There are some men who are admirable and worthy and loving." Tears misted her eyes and she blinked them back.

Chloe's lips parted. "You love him." Shock filled her tone.

Philippa managed a nod.

"Then why don't you—"

"It is done, Chloe."

"But—"

"I said, it is done," she said with a firmness and, for the first time, unwavering and so bold that Chloe fell silent. She would not debate all the reasons she could never be a wife to Miles. There was no greater personal hell than being so failed by one's body. And unless a person had lived with the agony of that in the loss of a child and in the death of a pregnancy, then they could never, ever know that pain.

Except, this was Chloe. "If you do love him, however, then nothing else should matter, Philippa."

Her lips twisted with bitterness. Yes, in the world of fairytales and make-believes, that was very much true. But this was her reality, and this was life, and there could be no rewriting it for that very reason. She gave thanks when another knock sounded at the door. She stepped to the door, opening the panel to admit two footmen, who gathered her trunks.

Not wanting any more questions or urgings from her sister, or anyone, she started out the door. Her sister hurried after her; adjusting her stride to match Philippa's quicker pace. "I am going to gather Faith and Violet," she said. "You go along without me."

"They are already belowstairs." She paused. "In the Ivory Parlor."

Philippa adjusted direction and started for the parlor. As she turned down the hall, the peel of her daughters' laughter spilled into the corridor and she managed her first real smile since last evening. With all the pain and despair that came with life, her daughters' joy had long proven a balm. She reached the edge of the doorway and then jerked to a stop as a familiar baritone sounded from inside the room. Her heart slowed and then sped up. Philippa rushed forward and then stopped. Miles knelt beside Faith and Violet, saying something that roused giggles from the sisters. They looked up at Philippa. The potent emotion pouring from Miles' gaze froze the air in her lungs.

"Mama," Faith exclaimed, shattering the moment. "Look." She held up a small bouquet of yellow buttercups. "Look what Miles brought me and Violet."

"Flow-ra" Violet shook her gift wildly and then hurled it at Miles. It hit his chest. With a grin, he ruffled the top of Violet's head.

Oh, God. How effortless he was with her daughters. How good and gentle and all things wonderful. Her lower lip quivered.

"Aren't they beautiful?" Faith chimed in happily.

"Most beautiful," she said past a tight throat. Miles climbed to his feet and her eyes went to the small bouquet of buttercups in his hand.

"Those ones are for you, Mama," Faith exclaimed, pointing at the flowers. "He even picked them himself, he said." She swung her gaze up to the silent gentleman beside her. "Isn't that right, Miles?"

He stretched his hand out. "Indeed. I had a most excellent tutor," he said and her heart twisted under the beautiful sweetness of that acknowledgement.

"Faith, take Violet and find Miss Cynthia."

Chest puffed with girlish pride, Faith collected her sister's hand. "Come along, Violet." The girls waved and then with a final good-bye to Miles, left.

Philippa smoothed her palms over her skirts.

"You were going to leave." His was a gruff accusation more than anything and still she nodded.

A flash of hurt glinted in his eyes and twisted the guilt deep inside her. "It is for the best." Surely he saw that?

"Why?" he shot back, striding over.

She looked blankly at him. Surely, given the scandal gracing the pages he had to see she had no place in London. Miles held his buttercup offering out and she accepted them with tremulous fingers. Philippa raised them to her nose and inhaled their sweet, fragrant scent.

Miles fished around the front of his jacket and brandished a thick, ivory vellum sheet. "It is a special license from the archbishop." The flowers slipped from her fingers and sailed into a soft, noiseless heap beside them. "Marry me."

"You don't have to—"

He slashed the air with his hand. When he spoke, his words were steeped in impatience. "This is not about what transpired last evening." And what now littered every scandal sheet in London. "This is about me, asking you to not leave with your family, but to remain here. With me." He held her gaze squarely. "Marry me."

And just like that, he held out every gift she'd never believed possible for herself. "Miles," she said, her voice hoarse with emotion. How did he not see that in being here, he was taking apart her heart?

"Please," he added, the faint entreaty reaching inside her.

She closed her eyes a moment. "I cannot," she said with an aching regret, which knifed away at her insides. "I—"

"I love you," he said.

The air left her on a swift exhale and Philippa pressed a palm against her mouth.

"I love you," he said cupping her cheek with infinite gentleness and she leaned into his caress. "And if I were skilled in verse, I'd offer you the pretty words you deserve."

"I never needed sonnets and poems," she said achingly.

"But you deserved them, anyway," he rasped, stuffing the special license in his jacket front. "If you reject my offer because you do not love me, I can accept that with the hope you will find a man deserving of you, who earns the gift of your heart."

A sound of protest stuck in her throat. How could he not know that he was the only man her heart would ever beat for? "I love you," she whispered. "And that is why I cannot marry you." A tear slipped down her cheek. Followed by another. And another. He caught them with the pad of his thumb, dusting away the remnants of her sadness. "There will come a time when you require your heir, Miles—"

"My mother had no right speaking to you about what I required." Oh, God. He knew that. "I do not require an heir," he bit out. "My brother can carry on the blasted bloodline."

"Then want one," she amended. "You will want one." For isn't that what all gentlemen ultimately wanted?

"Oh, Philippa," he said, his words husky. He cupped her cheeks in his hands. "Do you truly believe I would ever think an heir more important than your life?" He passed his strident gaze over her face. "There do not have to be babes. There are precautions I will take. I would neither want nor ask you to risk your life for that. You are all I want. You, Violet, and Faith."

A shuddery sob spilled past her lips. Oh, God. How was it possible to love him any more than she already did? And yet...in this moment, she fell in love with him all over again. Tears flooded her eyes. She wanted to be selfish and she wanted to take what he offered, and spit in the face of his mother, and all Societal conventions. But she could not. "You deserve more."

He pressed his forehead against hers and released a painful laugh. "Do not decide for me what I need or deserve. You *are* more. You are everything. I want you. I love *you*. And I will love your daughters as if they are mine and you three will be all I ever need."

Her shoulders shook with the force of her silent tears. For so many years she'd been taught to believe she served one purpose so that she'd come to believe it—until now. Now, with Miles promising her his heart and forever, putting her before all, he gave her the one gift she'd thought to never know. But the doubts lingered... she wet her lips. "You are certain? You—?"

Miles took her mouth under his in an aching kiss and then drew back. "I love you," he whispered, his breath fanning her lips. "Marry me?" he asked, once more. "Let me spend the rest of our lives showing you the happiness you have been so robbed of."

As the years' worth of self-doubt and purposelessness lifted, she was filled with a buoyant light. Philippa touched the necklace at her throat. "There is something I must do," she said softly.

His arms fell uselessly at his side. The muscles of his throat moved. She smiled slowly. "I must inform my family that we cannot leave yet." He went still. "Not until at least after our wedding." And as Miles took her lips under his once more, warmth suffused every corner of her person.

After years of having given up on happiness for herself, it seemed she'd been wrong—happily-ever-afters did exist.

EPILOGUE

Sussex, England
One month later

"WHAT IS IT? *Pleeease,* TELL me," Faith pleaded, as she walked between Philippa and Miles through the gardens of their Sussex estate.

Miles set aside the picnic basket and snapped open a white sheet. It fluttered in the early summer breeze and then he laid it down on the ground. "Soon," he promised.

"Soon. Soon." Violet parroted back and, squealing, all but leapt from Philippa's embrace into Miles'.

As he took the small girl in his arms and tossed her into the air laughing, easily catching her, Philippa stared on. Warmth swelled in her breast. And just as she'd fallen in love with Miles Brookfield, the Marquess of Guilford, that day in Hyde Park just over one month earlier, she fell in love with him all over again in the gardens of their country estate.

Faith turned to Philippa and pleaded with her eyes. "What is the present, Mama?"

Over the top of Violet's head, Miles held Philippa's gaze. He flashed her a secretive smile that caused a familiar fluttering in her belly. *I love you,* he mouthed. She touched quivering fingers to her breast. *I love you,* she returned.

"Mama?" Faith tugged at her skirts again.

"I am afraid I do not know what surprise Miles has for us." And she didn't. She knew nothing more than his calls for a picnic outside in the gardens where he would give Philippa, Faith, and Violet a very special gift.

"Is no one ready for a present?" Miles asked. Shifting Violet to the nook of his right arm, he used his spare hand to scratch at his forehead.

An excited squeal escaped Faith. "I am ready, Miles."

He set Violet down and her older sister rushed to claim a spot beside her. Violet bounced up and down, clapping. "Ready."

"This is a very special gift," Miles told them in solemn tones. His tender effort to always present his mouth so Faith could see caused tears to blur Philippa's vision. She blinked them back and found him studying her. "All my special ladies must be here." He held his hand up for Philippa.

She allowed him to help her down to the spot beside him and as he turned his attention to the basket and fished out three small packages, her curiosity piqued. No one had ever given her a gift. Her late husband hadn't cared enough about her to know her interests. Her family had been so mired down in simply surviving that those whimsical pleasures had escaped them.

Miles handed a small, wrapped package to each lady.

They stared expectantly back.

"Well, open them," he urged. "They are yours."

Faith tore into the soft wrap, as Miles helped Violet through the fine movements in opening hers. Philippa attended her package.

"Books, Mama," Faith cried, waving around the small, thin, leather bound book. "He bought us each a book."

"The *same* book," Miles clarified.

Faith tipped her head. "The same?"

A gentle breeze wafted about them, tugging at the edge of the blanket. "Yes. For you see, this is not just any book," he continued in those hushed tones that always managed to capture even Violet's fleeting attention. "This is a *special* fairytale about a princess who was lost in a park."

Dropping her attention to the leather book, Philippa opened it and her gaze snagged on the title. *Our Story*. Her heart started.

"The princess was lost like me," Faith piped in.

"Like you," he confirmed. "And this princess had a laughing, loving sister."

"Violet," Faith exclaimed.

Violet tossed her book aside and scrambled onto Miles' lap.

Oh, God. Her fingers shaking, Philippa set aside the treasure he'd given them. Just one more beautiful gift. Her heart swelled.

"And these two princesses had a strong, courageous mother." His voice hoarsened by emotion, Miles stretched a hand out and, wordlessly, Philippa slid her palm into his. The same heat that always burned at his touch went through her. "This mother was brave and beautiful in every way."

Scrambling up onto her knees, Faith rushed over to Miles and clung to his shoulder. "Does the prince become a papa to them, like you are to me and Violet?"

Philippa buried a little sob in her fist, as he gently brushed a dark curl from Faith's brow.

"He does," he said quietly.

Faith took Miles' face between her hands. "It is the perfect gift, Papa."

The column of his throat worked.

Papa. For so long, Philippa had believed a nobleman incapable of seeing a child. She'd believed the tenderness Miles had shown Faith and Violet an elusive dream only recorded in fanciful tales. Until Miles. How much he'd shown her about love and life.

An orange-winged butterfly floated by and Violet wiggled off Miles' lap and toddled over to it. "I touch it. I touch it." As the little girl ambled over to the fluttering creature, Faith surged to her feet with a laugh and set out in chase.

Miles scooted over to Philippa's side so they were shoulder to shoulder, staring out at their girls. "It is our story," Philippa whispered. "You wrote our story." A tear slid down her cheek and he turned and caught the drop with his thumb, flicking it away.

"You once told me that you'd ceased to believe in fairytales." Gathering her fingers in his, Miles raised her knuckles to his lips and placed a lingering kiss that sent shivers radiating. "I wanted to gift you and our daughters with something to forever remind you of my love. A gift to remind each of you that fairytales are very much real."

Another tear slid down her cheek. Followed by another. "Oh,

Miles." She shifted so they faced one another and worked her gaze lovingly over the planes of his face. "How can you not know?"

He shook his head.

Philippa rested her brow against his. "Together, *you*, Violet, and Faith, are the only gifts I ever wanted or needed, Miles. You showed me all those dreams are possible."

The wind tossed one of his ginger strands over his eye. "Then let us write the rest of our story together."

And with their daughters' laughter ringing in the gardens, Philippa claimed his lips in a kiss, knowing that is just what they would do.

The End

OTHER BOOKS BY CHRISTI CALDWELL

TO ENCHANT A WICKED DUKE
Book 13 in the "Heart of a Duke" Series by Christi Caldwell

A Devil in Disguise

Years ago, when Nick Tallings, the recent Duke of Huntly, watched his family destroyed at the hands of a merciless nobleman, he vowed revenge. But his efforts had been futile, as his enemy, Lord Rutland is without weakness.

Until now…

With his rival finally happily married, Nick is able to set his ruthless scheme into motion. His plot hinges upon Lord Rutland's innocent, empty-headed sister-in-law, Justina Barrett. Nick will ruin her, marry her, and then leave her brokenhearted.

A Lady Dreaming of Love

From the moment Justina Barrett makes her Come Out, she is labeled a Diamond. Even with her ruthless father determined to sell her off to the highest bidder, Justina never gives up on her hope for a good, honorable gentleman who values her wit more than her looks.

A Not-So-Chance Meeting

Nick's ploy to ensnare Justina falls neatly into place in the streets of London. With each carefully orchestrated encounter, he slips further and further inside the lady's heart, never anticipating that Justina, with her quick wit and strength, will break down his own defenses. As Nick's plans begins to unravel, he's left to determine which is more important—Justina's love or his vow for vengeance. But can Justina ever forgive the duke who deceived her?

ONE WINTER WITH A BARON
Book 12 in the "Heart of a Duke" Series by Christi Caldwell

A clever spinster:
Content with her spinster lifestyle, Miss Sybil Cunning wants to prove that a future as an unmarried woman is the only life for her. As a bluestocking who values hard, empirical data, Sybil needs help with her research. Nolan Pratt, Baron Webb, one of society's most scandalous rakes, is the perfect gentleman to help her. After all, he inspires fear in proper mothers and desire within their daughters.
A notorious rake:
Society may be aware of Nolan Pratt, Baron's Webb's wicked ways, but what he has carefully hidden is his miserable handling of his family's finances. When Sybil presents him the opportunity to earn much-needed funds, he can't refuse.
A winter to remember:
However, what begins as a business arrangement becomes something more and with every meeting, Sybil slips inside his heart. Can this clever woman look beneath the veneer of a coldhearted rake to see the man Nolan truly is?

TO REDEEM A RAKE
Book 11 in the "Heart of a Duke" Series by Christi Caldwell

He's spent years scandalizing society.
Now, this rake must change his ways.

Society's most infamous scoundrel, Daniel Winterbourne, the Earl of Montfort, has been promised a small fortune if he can relinquish his wayward, carousing lifestyle. And behaving means he must also help find a respectable companion for his youngest sister—someone who will guide her and whom she can emulate. However, Daniel knows no such woman. But when he encounters a childhood friend, Daniel believes she may just be the answer to all of his problems.

Having been secretly humiliated by an unscrupulous blackguard years earlier, Miss Daphne Smith dreams of finding work at Ladies of Hope, an institution that provides an education for disabled women. With her sordid past and a disfigured leg, few opportunities arise for a woman such as she. Knowing Daniel's history, she wishes to avoid him, but working for his sister is exactly the stepping stone she needs.

Their attraction intensifies as Daniel and Daphne grow closer, preparing his sister for the London Season. But Daniel must resist his desire for a woman tarnished by scandal while Daphne is reminded of the boy she once knew. Can society's most notorious rake redeem his reputation and become the man Daphne deserves?

To Woo a Widow
Book 10 in the "Heart of a Duke" Series by Christi Caldwell

They see a brokenhearted widow.
She's far from shattered.

Lady Philippa Winston is never marrying again. After her late husband's cruelty that she kept so well hidden, she has no desire to search for love.

Years ago, Miles Brookfield, the Marquess of Guilford, made a frivolous vow he never thought would come to fruition—he promised to marry his mother's goddaughter if he was unwed by the age of thirty. Now, to his dismay, he's faced with honoring that pledge. But when he encounters the beautiful and intriguing Lady Philippa, Miles knows his true path in life. It's up to him to break down every belief Philippa carries about gentlemen, proving that not only is love real, but that he is the man deserving of her sheltered heart.

Will Philippa let down her guard and allow Miles to woo a widow in desperate need of his love?

THE LURE OF A RAKE
Book 9 in the "Heart of a Duke" Series by Christi Caldwell

A Lady Dreaming of Love

Lady Genevieve Farendale has a scandalous past. Jilted at the altar years earlier and exiled by her family, she's now returned to London to prove she can be a proper lady. Even though she's not given up on the hope of marrying for love, she's wary of trusting again. Then she meets Cedric Falcot, the Marquess of St. Albans whose seductive ways set her heart aflutter. But with her sordid history, Genevieve knows a rake can also easily destroy her.

An Unlikely Pairing

What begins as a chance encounter between Cedric and Genevieve becomes something more. As they continue to meet, passions stir. But with Genevieve's hope for true love, she fears Cedric will be unable to give up his wayward lifestyle. After all, Cedric has spent years protecting his heart, and keeping everyone out. Slowly, she chips away at all the walls he's built, but when he falters, Genevieve can't offer him redemption. Now, it's up to Cedric to prove to Genevieve that the love of a man is far more powerful than the lure of a rake.

TO TRUST A ROGUE
Book 8 in the "Heart of a Duke" Series by Christi Caldwell

A rogue

Marcus, the Viscount Wessex has carefully crafted the image of rogue and charmer for Polite Society. Under that façade, however, dwells a man whose dreams were shattered almost eight years earlier by a young lady who captured his heart, pledged her love, and then left him, with nothing more than a curt note.

A widow

Eight years earlier, faced with no other choice, Mrs. Eleanor Collins, fled London and the only man she ever loved, Marcus, Viscount Wessex. She has now returned to serve as a companion for her elderly aunt with a daughter in tow. Even though they're next door neighbors, there is little reason for her to move in the same circles as Marcus, just in case, she vows to avoid him, for he reminds her of all she lost when she left.

Reunited

As their paths continue to cross, Marcus finds his desire for Eleanor just as strong, but he learned long ago she's not to be trusted. He will offer her a place in his bed, but not anything more. Only, Eleanor has no interest in this new, roguish man. The more time they spend together, the protective wall they've constructed to keep the other out, begin to break. With all the betrayals and secrets between them, Marcus has to open his heart again. And Eleanor must decide if it's ever safe to trust a rogue.

To Wed His Christmas Lady
Book 7 in the "Heart of a Duke" Series by Christi Caldwell

She's longing to be loved:

Lady Cara Falcot has only served one purpose to her loathsome father—to increase his power through a marriage to the future Duke of Billingsley. As such, she's built protective walls about her heart, and presents an icy facade to the world around her. Journeying home from her finishing school for the Christmas holidays, Cara's carriage is stranded during a winter storm. She's forced to tarry at a ramshackle inn, where she immediately antagonizes another patron—William.

He's avoiding his duty in favor of one last adventure:

William Hargrove, the Marquess of Grafton has wanted only one thing in life—to avoid the future match his parents would have him make to a cold, duke's daughter. He's returning home from a blissful eight years of traveling the world to see to his responsibilities. But when a winter storm interrupts his trip and lands him at a falling-down inn, he's forced to share company with a commanding Lady Cara who initially reminds him exactly of the woman he so desperately wants to avoid.

A Christmas snowstorm ushers in the spirit of the season:

At the holiday time, these two people who despise each other due to first perceptions are offered renewed beginnings and fresh starts. As this gruff stranger breaks down the walls she's built about herself, Cara has to determine whether she can truly open her heart to trusting that any man is capable of good and that she herself is capable of love. And William has to set aside all previous thoughts he's carried of the polished ladies like Cara, to be the man to show her that love.

THE HEART OF A SCOUNDREL
Book 6 in the "Heart of a Duke" Series by Christi Caldwell

Ruthless, wicked, and dark, the Marquess of Rutland rouses terror in the breast of ladies and nobleman alike. All Edmund wants in life is power. After he was publically humiliated by his one love Lady Margaret, he vowed vengeance, using Margaret's niece, as his pawn. Except, he's thwarted by another, more enticing target—Miss Phoebe Barrett.

Miss Phoebe Barrett knows precisely the shame she's been born to. Because her father is a shocking letch she's learned to form her own opinions on a person's worth. After a chance meeting with the Marquess of Rutland, she is captivated by the mysterious man. He, too, is a victim of society's scorn, but the more encounters she has with Edmund, the more she knows there is powerful depth and emotion to the jaded marquess.

The lady wreaks havoc on Edmund's plans for revenge and he finds he wants Phoebe, at all costs. As she's drawn into the darkness of his world, Phoebe risks being destroyed by Edmund's ruthlessness. And Phoebe who desires love at all costs, has to determine if she can ever truly trust the heart of a scoundrel.

To Love a Lord
Book 5 in the "Heart of a Duke" Series by Christi Caldwell

All she wants is security:

The last place finishing school instructor Mrs. Jane Munroe belongs, is in polite Society. Vowing to never wed, she's been scuttled around from post to post. Now she finds herself in the Marquess of Waverly's household. She's never met a nobleman she liked, and when she meets the pompous, arrogant marquess, she remembers why. But soon, she discovers Gabriel is unlike any gentleman she's ever known.

All he wants is a companion for his sister:

What Gabriel finds himself with instead, is a fiery spirited, bespectacled woman who entices him at every corner and challenges his age-old vow to never trust his heart to a woman. But... there is something suspicious about his sister's companion. And he is determined to find out just what it is.

All they need is each other:

As Gabriel and Jane confront the truth of their feelings, the lies and secrets between them begin to unravel. And Jane is left to decide whether or not it is ever truly safe to love a lord.

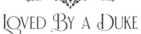

Loved By a Duke
Book 4 in the "Heart of a Duke" Series by Christi Caldwell

For ten years, Lady Daisy Meadows has been in love with Auric, the Duke of Crawford. Ever since his gallant rescue years earlier, Daisy knew she was destined to be his Duchess. Unfortunately, Auric sees her as his best friend's sister and nothing more. But perhaps, if she can manage to find the fabled heart of a duke pendant, she will win over the heart of her duke.

Auric, the Duke of Crawford enjoys Daisy's company. The last thing he is interested in however, is pursuing a romance with a woman he's known since she was in leading strings. This season, Daisy is turning up in the oddest places and he cannot help but notice that she is no longer a girl. But Auric wouldn't do something as foolhardy as to fall in love with Daisy. He couldn't. Not with the guilt he carries over his past sins… Not when he has no right to her heart…But perhaps, just perhaps, she can forgive the past and trust that he'd forever cherish her heart—but will she let him?

THE LOVE OF A ROGUE
Book 3 in the "Heart of a Duke" Series by Christi Caldwell

Lady Imogen Moore hasn't had an easy time of it since she made her Come Out. With her betrothed, a powerful duke breaking it off to wed her sister, she's become the *tons* favorite piece of gossip. Never again wanting to experience the pain of a broken heart, she's resolved to make a match with a polite, respectable gentleman. The last thing she wants is another reckless rogue.

Lord Alex Edgerton has a problem. His brother, tired of Alex's carousing has charged him with chaperoning their remaining, unwed sister about *ton* events. Shopping? No, thank you. Attending the theatre? He'd rather be at Forbidden Pleasures with a scantily clad beauty upon his lap. The task of *chaperone* becomes even more of a bother when his sister drags along her dearest friend, Lady Imogen to social functions. The last thing he wants in his life is a young, innocent English miss.

Except, as Alex and Imogen are thrown together, passions flare and Alex comes to find he not only wants Imogen in his bed, but also in his heart. Yet now he must convince Imogen to risk all, on the heart of a rogue.

MORE THAN A DUKE
Book 2 in the "Heart of a Duke" Series by Christi Caldwell

Polite Society doesn't take Lady Anne Adamson seriously. However, Anne isn't just another pretty young miss. When she discovers her father betrayed her mother's love and her family descended into poverty, Anne comes up with a plan to marry a respectable, powerful, and honorable gentleman—a man nothing like her philandering father.

Armed with the heart of a duke pendant, fabled to land the wearer a duke's heart, she decides to enlist the aid of the notorious Harry, 6th Earl of Stanhope. A scoundrel with a scandalous past, he is the last gentleman she'd ever wed...however, his reputation marks him the perfect man to school her in the art of seduction so she might ensnare the illustrious Duke of Crawford.

Harry, the Earl of Stanhope is a jaded, cynical rogue who lives for his own pleasures. Having been thrown over by the only woman he ever loved so she could wed a duke, he's not at all surprised when Lady Anne approaches him with her scheme to capture another duke's affection. He's come to appreciate that all women are in fact greedy, title-grasping, self-indulgent creatures. And with Anne's history of grating on his every last nerve, she is the last woman he'd ever agree to school in the art of seduction. Only his friendship with the lady's sister compels him to help.

What begins as a pretend courtship, born of lessons on seduction, becomes something more leaving Anne to decide if she can give her heart to a reckless rogue, and Harry must decide if he's willing to again trust in a lady's love.

FOR LOVE OF THE DUKE
First Full-Length Book in the "Heart of a Duke" Series
by Christi Caldwell

After the tragic death of his wife, Jasper, the 8th Duke of Bainbridge buried himself away in the dark cold walls of his home, Castle Blackwood. When he's coaxed out of his self-imposed exile to attend the amusements of the Frost Fair, his life is irrevocably changed by his fateful meeting with Lady Katherine Adamson.

With her tight brown ringlets and silly white-ruffled gowns, Lady Katherine Adamson has found her dance card empty for two Seasons. After her father's passing, Katherine learned the unreliability of men, and is determined to depend on no one, except herself. Until she meets Jasper...

In a desperate bid to avoid a match arranged by her family, Katherine makes the Duke of Bainbridge a shocking proposition—one that he accepts.

Only, as Katherine begins to love Jasper, she finds the arrangement agreed upon is not enough. And Jasper is left to decide if protecting his heart is more important than fighting for Katherine's love.

IN NEED OF A DUKE
A Prequel Novella to "The Heart of a Duke" Series
by Christi Caldwell

In Need of a Duke: (Author's Note: This is a prequel novella to "The Heart of a Duke" series by Christi Caldwell. It was originally available in "The Heart of a Duke" Collection and is now being published as an individual novella.

~★~

It features a new prologue and epilogue.

Years earlier, a gypsy woman passed to Lady Aldora Adamson and her friends a heart pendant that promised them each the heart of a duke.

Now, a young lady, with her family facing ruin and scandal, Lady Aldora doesn't have time for mythical stories about cheap baubles. She needs to save her sisters and brother by marrying a titled gentleman with wealth and power to his name. She sets her bespectacled sights upon the Marquess of St. James.

Turned out by his father after a tragic scandal, Lord Michael Knightly has grown into a powerful, but self-made man. With the whispers and stares that still follow him, he would rather be anywhere but London...

Until he meets Lady Aldora, a young woman who mistakes him for his brother, the Marquess of St. James. The connection between Aldora and Michael is immediate and as they come to know one another, Aldora's feelings for Michael war with her sisterly responsibilities. With her family's dire situation, a man of Michael's scandalous past will never do.

Ultimately, Aldora must choose between her responsibilities as a sister and her love for Michael.

ONCE A WALLFLOWER, AT LAST HIS LOVE
Book 6 in the Scandalous Seasons Series

Responsible, practical Miss Hermione Rogers, has been crafting stories as the notorious Mr. Michael Michaelmas and selling them for a meager wage to support her siblings. The only real way to ensure her family's ruinous debts are paid, however, is to marry. Tall, thin, and plain, she has no expectation of success. In London for her first Season she seizes the chance to write the tale of a brooding duke. In her research, she finds Sebastian Fitzhugh, the 5th Duke of Mallen, who unfortunately is perfectly affable, charming, and so nicely... configured... he takes her breath away. He lacks all the character traits she needs for her story, but alas, any duke will have to do.

Sebastian Fitzhugh, the 5th Duke of Mallen has been deceived so many times during the high-stakes game of courtship, he's lost faith in Society women. Yet, after a chance encounter with Hermione, he finds himself intrigued. Not a woman he'd normally consider beautiful, the young lady's practical bent, her forthright nature and her tendency to turn up in the oddest places has his interests… roused. He'd like to trust her, he'd like to do a whole lot more with her too, but should he?

A Marquess For Christmas
Book 5 in the Scandalous Seasons Series

Lady Patrina Tidemore gave up on the ridiculous notion of true love after having her heart shattered and her trust destroyed by a black-hearted cad. Used as a pawn in a game of revenge against her brother, Patrina returns to London from a failed elopement with a tattered reputation and little hope for a respectable match. The only peace she finds is in her solitude on the cold winter days at Hyde Park. And even that is yanked from her by two little hellions who just happen to have a devastatingly handsome, but coldly aloof father, the Marquess of Beaufort. Something about the lord stirs the dreams she'd once carried for an honorable gentleman's love.

Weston Aldridge, the 4th Marquess of Beaufort was deceived and betrayed by his late wife. In her faithlessness, he's come to view women as self-serving, indulgent creatures. Except, after a series of chance encounters with Patrina, he comes to appreciate how uniquely different she is than all women he's ever known.

At the Christmastide season, a time of hope and new beginnings, Patrina and Weston, unexpectedly learn true love in one another. However, as Patrina's scandalous past threatens their future and the happiness of his children, they are both left to determine if love is enough.

Always a Rogue, Forever Her Love
Book 4 in the Scandalous Seasons Series

Miss Juliet Marshville is spitting mad. With one guardian missing, and the other singularly uninterested in her fate, she is at the mercy of her wastrel brother who loses her beloved childhood home to a man known as Sin. Determined to reclaim control of Rosecliff Cottage and her own fate, Juliet arranges a meeting with the notorious rogue and demands the return of her property.

Jonathan Tidemore, 5th Earl of Sinclair, known to the *ton* as Sin, is exceptionally lucky in life and at the gaming tables. He has just one problem. Well…four, really. His incorrigible sisters have driven off yet another governess. This time, however, his mother demands he find an appropriate replacement.

When Miss Juliet Marshville boldly demands the return of her precious cottage, he takes advantage of his sudden good fortune and puts an offer to her; turn his sisters into proper English ladies, and he'll return Rosecliff Cottage to Juliet's possession.

Jonathan comes to appreciate Juliet's spirit, courage, and clever wit, and decides to claim the fiery beauty as his mistress. Juliet, however, will be mistress for no man. Nor could she ever love a man who callously stole her home in a game of cards. As Jonathan begins to see Juliet as more than a spirited beauty to warm his bed, he realizes she could be a lady he could love the rest of his life, if only he can convince the proud Juliet that he's worthy of her hand and heart.

Always Proper, Suddenly Scandalous
Book 3 in the Scandalous Seasons Series

Geoffrey Winters, Viscount Redbrooke was not always the hard, unrelenting lord driven by propriety. After a tragic mistake, he resolved to honor his responsibility to the Redbrooke line and live a life, free of scandal. Knowing his duty is to wed a proper, respectable English miss, he selects Lady Beatrice Dennington, daughter of the Duke of Somerset, the perfect woman for him. Until he meets Miss Abigail Stone…

To distance herself from a personal scandal, Abigail Stone flees America to visit her uncle, the Duke of Somerset. Determined to never trust a man again, she is helplessly intrigued by the hard, too-proper Geoffrey. With his strict appreciation for decorum and order, he is nothing like the man' she's always dreamed of.

Abigail is everything Geoffrey does not need. She upends his carefully ordered world at every encounter. As they begin to care for one another, Abigail carefully guards the secret that resulted in her journey to England.

Only, if Geoffrey learns the truth about Abigail, he must decide which he holds most dear: his place in Society or Abigail's place in his heart.

Never Courted, Suddenly Wed
Book 2 in the Scandalous Seasons Series

Christopher Ansley, Earl of Waxham, has constructed a perfect image for the *ton*–the ladies love him and his company is desired by all. Only two people know the truth about Waxham's secret. Unfortunately, one of them is Miss Sophie Winters.

Sophie Winters has known Christopher since she was in leading strings. As children, they delighted in tormenting each other. Now at two and twenty, she still has a tendency to find herself in scrapes, and her marital prospects are slim.

When his father threatens to expose his shame to the *ton*, unless he weds Sophie for her dowry, Christopher concocts a plan to remain a bachelor. What he didn't plan on was falling in love with the lively, impetuous Sophie. As secrets are exposed, will Christopher's love be enough when she discovers his role in his father's scheme?

FOREVER BETROTHED, NEVER THE BRIDE
Book 1 in the Scandalous Seasons Series

Hopeless romantic Lady Emmaline Fitzhugh is tired of sitting with the wallflowers, waiting for her betrothed to come to his senses and marry her. When Emmaline reads one too many reports of his scandalous liaisons in the gossip rags, she takes matters into her own hands.

War-torn veteran Lord Drake devotes himself to forgetting his days on the Peninsula through an endless round of meaningless associations. He no longer wants to feel anything, but Lady Emmaline is making it hard to maintain a state of numbness. With her zest for life, she awakens his passion and desire for love.

The one woman Drake has spent the better part of his life avoiding is now the only woman he needs, but he is no longer a man worthy of his Emmaline. It is up to her to show him the healing power of love.

A SEASON OF HOPE
A Danby Novella

Five years ago when her love, Marcus Wheatley, failed to return from fighting Napoleon's forces, Lady Olivia Foster buried her heart. Unable to betray Marcus's memory, Olivia has gone out of her way to run off prospective suitors. At three and twenty she considers herself firmly on the shelf. Her father, however, disagrees and accepts an offer for Olivia's hand in marriage. Yet it's Christmas, when anything can happen…

Olivia receives a well-timed summons from her grandfather, the Duke of Danby, and eagerly embraces the reprieve from her betrothal.

Only, when Olivia arrives at Danby Castle she realizes the Christmas season represents hope, second chances, and even miracles.

"Winning a Lady's Heart"
A Danby Novella

Author's Note: This is a novella that was originally available in A Summons From The Castle (The Regency Christmas Summons Collection). It is being published as an individual novella.

~★~

For Lady Alexandra, being the source of a cold, calculated wager is bad enough...but when it is waged by Nathaniel Michael Winters, 5th Earl of Pembroke, the man she's in love with, it results in a broken heart, the scandal of the season, and a summons from her grandfather – the Duke of Danby.

To escape Society's gossip, she hurries to her meeting with the duke, determined to put memories of the earl far behind. Except the duke has other plans for Alexandra...plans which include the 5th Earl of Pembroke!

Tempted by a Lady's Smile
Book 4 in the "Lords of Honor" Series

Richard Jonas has loved but one woman—a woman who belongs to his brother. Refusing to suffer any longer, he evades his family in order to barricade his heart from unrequited love. While attending a friend's summer party, Richard's approach to love is changed after sharing a passionate and life-altering kiss with a vibrant and mysterious woman. Believing he was incapable of loving again, Richard finds himself tempted by a young lady determined to marry his best friend.

Gemma Reed has not been treated kindly by the *ton*. Often disregarded for her appearance and interests unlike those of a proper lady, Gemma heads to house party to win the heart of Lord Westfield, the man she's loved for years. But her plan is set off course by the tempting and intriguing, Richard Jonas.

A chance meeting creates a new path for Richard and Gemma to forage—but can two people, scorned and shunned by those they've loved from afar, let down their guards to find true happiness?

"RESCUED BY A LADY'S LOVE"
Book 3 in the "Lords of Honor" Series

Destitute and determined to finally be free of any man's shackles, Lily Benedict sets out to salvage her honor. With no choice but to commit a crime that will save her from her past, she enters the home of the recluse, Derek Winters, the new Duke of Blackthorne. But entering the "Beast of Blackthorne's" lair proves more threatening than she ever imagined.

With half a face and a mangled leg, Derek—once rugged and charming—only exists within the confines of his home. Shunned by society, Derek is leery of the hauntingly beautiful Lily Benedict. As time passes, she slips past his defenses, reminding him how to live again. But when Lily's sordid past comes back, threatening her life, it's up to Derek to find the strength to become the hero he once was. Can they overcome the darkness of their sins to find a life of love and redemption?

CAPTIVATED BY A LADY'S CHARM
Book 2 in the "Lords of Honor" Series

In need of a wife…

Christian Villiers, the Marquess of St. Cyr, despises the role he's been cast into as fortune hunter but requires the funds to keep his marquisate solvent. Yet, the sins of his past cloud his future, preventing him from seeing beyond his fateful actions at the Battle of Toulouse. For he knows inevitably it will catch up with him, and everyone will remember his actions on the battlefield that cost so many so much—particularly his best friend.

In want of a husband...

Lady Prudence Tidemore's life is plagued by familial scandals, which makes her own marital prospects rather grim. Surely there is one gentleman of the ton who can look past her family and see just her and all she has to offer?

When Prudence runs into Christian on a London street, the charming, roguish gentleman immediately captures her attention. But then a chance meeting becomes a waltz, and now...

A Perfect Match...

All she must do is convince Christian to forget the cold requirements he has for his future marchioness. But the demons in his past prevent him from turning himself over to love. One thing is certain—Prudence wants the marquess and is determined to have him in her life, now and forever. It's just a matter of convincing Christian he wants the same.

SEDUCED BY A LADY'S HEART
Book 1 in the "Lords of Honor" Series

You met Lieutenant Lucien Jones in "Forever Betrothed, Never the Bride" when he was a broken soldier returned from fighting Boney's forces. This is his story of triumph and happily-ever-after!

~★~

Lieutenant Lucien Jones, son of a viscount, returned from war, to find his wife and child dead. Blaming his father for the commission that sent him off to fight Boney's forces, he was content to languish at London Hospital... until offered employment on the Marquess of Drake's staff. Through his position, Lucien found purpose in life and is content to keep his past buried.

Lady Eloise Yardley has loved Lucien since they were children. Having long ago given up on the dream of him, she married another. Years later, she is a young, lonely widow who does not fit in with the ton. When Lucien's family enlists her aid to reunite father and son, she leaps at the opportunity to not only aid her former friend, but to also escape London.

Lucien doesn't know what scheme Eloise has concocted, but

knowing her as he does, when she pays a visit to his employer, he knows she's up to something. The last thing he wants is the temptation that this new, older, mature Eloise presents; a tantalizing reminder of happier times and peace.

Yet Eloise is determined to win Lucien's love once and for all... if only Lucien can set aside the pain of his past and risk all on a lady's heart.

Only For Their Love
Book 3 in the "The Theodosia Sword" Series

Miss Carol Cresswall bore witness to her parents' loveless union and is determined to avoid that same miserable fate. Her mother has altogether different plans—plans that include a match between Carol and Lord Gregory Renshaw. Despite his wealth and power, Carol has no interest in marrying a pompous man who goes out of his way to ignore her. Now, with their families coming together for the Christmastide season it's her mother's last-ditch effort to get them together. And Carol plans to avoid Gregory at all costs.

Lord Gregory Renshaw has no intentions of falling prey to his mother's schemes to marry him off to a proper debutante she's picked out. Over the years, he has carefully sidestepped all endeavors to be matched with any of the grasping ladies.

But a sudden Christmastide Scandal has the potential show Carol and Gregory that they've spent years running from the one thing they've always needed.

Only For Her Honor
Book 2 in the "The Theodosia Sword" Series

A wounded soldier:

When Captain Lucas Rayne returned from fighting Boney's forces, he was a shell of a man. A recluse who doesn't leave his family's estate, he's content to shut himself away. Until he meets Eve…

A woman alone in the world:

Eve Ormond spent most of her life following the drum alongside her late father. When his shameful actions bring death and pain to English soldiers, Eve is forced back to England, an outcast. With no family or marital prospects she needs employment and finds it in Captain Lucas Rayne's home. A man whose life was ruined by her father, Eve has no place inside his household. With few options available, however, Eve takes the post. What she never anticipates is how with their every meeting, this honorable, hurting soldier slips inside her heart.

The Secrets Between Them:

The more time Lucas spends with Eve, he remembers what it is to be alive and he lets the walls protecting his heart down. When the secrets between them come to light will their love be enough? Or are they two destined for heartbreak?

Only For His Lady
Book 1 in the "The Theodosia Sword" Series

A curse. A sword. And the thief who stole her heart.

The Rayne family is trapped in a rut of bad luck. And now, it's up to Lady Theodosia Rayne to steal back the Theodosia sword, a gladius that was pilfered by the rival, loathed Renshaw family. Hopefully, recovering the stolen sword will break the cycle and reverse her family's fate.

Damian Renshaw, the Duke of Devlin, is feared by all—all, that is, except Lady Theodosia, the brazen spitfire who enters his home and wrestles an ancient relic from his wall. Intrigued by the vivacious woman, Devlin has no intentions of relinquishing the sword to her.

As Theodosia and Damian battle for ownership, passion ignites. Now, they are torn between their age-old feud and the fire that burns between them. Can two forbidden lovers find a way to make amends before their families' war tears them apart?

My Lady of Deception
Book 1 in the "Brethren of the Lords" Series

This dark, sweeping Regency novel was previously only offered as part of the limited edition box sets: "From the Ballroom and Beyond", "Romancing the Rogue", and "Dark Deceptions". Now, available for the first time on its own, exclusively through Amazon is "My Lady of Deception".

~★~

Everybody has a secret. Some are more dangerous than others.

For Georgina Wilcox, only child of the notorious traitor known as "The Fox", there are too many secrets to count. However, after her interference results in great tragedy, she resolves to never help another… until she meets Adam Markham.

Lord Adam Markham is captured by The Fox. Imprisoned, Adam loses everything he holds dear. As his days in captivity grow, he finds himself fascinated by the young maid, Georgina, who cares for him.

When the carefully crafted lies she's built between them begin to crumble, Georgina realizes she will do anything to prove her love and loyalty to Adam—even it means at the expense of her own life.

NON-FICTION WORKS BY
CHRISTI CALDWELL

**Uninterrupted Joy: Memoir: My Journey through
Infertility, Pregnancy, and Special Needs**

The following journey was never intended for publication. It was written from a mother, to her unborn child. The words detailed her struggle through infertility and the joy of finally being pregnant. A stunning revelation at her son's birth opened a world of both fear and discovery. This is the story of one mother's love and hope and…her quest for uninterrupted joy.

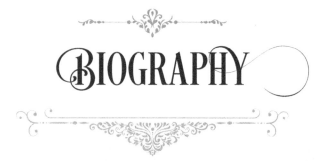

BIOGRAPHY

Christi Caldwell is the bestselling author of historical romance novels set in the Regency era. Christi blames Judith McNaught's "Whitney, My Love," for luring her into the world of historical romance. While sitting in her graduate school apartment at the University of Connecticut, Christi decided to set aside her notes and try her hand at writing romance. She believes the most perfect heroes and heroines have imperfections and rather enjoys tormenting them before crafting a well-deserved happily ever after!

When Christi isn't writing the stories of flawed heroes and heroines, she can be found in her Southern Connecticut home chasing around her eight-year-old son, and caring for twin princesses-in-training!

Visit *www.christicaldwellauthor.com* to learn more about what Christi is working on, or join her on Facebook at Christi Caldwell Author, and Twitter *@ChristiCaldwell*